DARK
SHADOW

DARK SHADOW

DARKHAVEN SAGA: BOOK SIX

DANIELLE ROSE

WATERHOUSE PRESS

For the readers—

Because without you,
there never would have been a sixth book.

ONE

It has been one month since we lost Amicia and Will, and ever since that night, there has been a shadow haunting me. It waits in the darkness, striking only when I take my first deep inhalation after weeks of holding my breath. It slithers like a snake, coiling its body around my torso, smothering me until I can bear it no more. It likes my pain, and the sick part is that I do too. The pain lets me know I am still alive.

I fall to the ground, my knees sinking into the freshly thawed earth. The wet tundra makes a squishing sound as I drop, and I squirm against the sensation. My jeans become moist where I meet the land, and as I shift in place, I make a greater mess of things. I continue to burrow, mud seeping at the forefront of my flesh, and I cringe.

I try to ignore all of these things, even though the sound of the earth's protest irritates my senses because I am not here to listen to the earth. I am here to see *him*. Will must capture my full attention, and I dare never to take it away from him.

I sigh, my breath coming in weak puffs as I try to calm my rapid heart. It burns in my chest, and my eyes sting from his loss. Even though many days have passed since he died in my arms, the pain never lessens. I imagine it never will. In the short time I knew Will, he made a mark on my heart. I feel his presence everywhere now, and it is a brutal reminder that he will never return.

"It has been four weeks," I whisper. "But I still visit every day since ... since—"

A sharp breath bursts through me, but with it, I find no reprieve from my emotions. I squeeze my eyes shut, hoping to cast out the memories that haunt me day after day. This never works, but I try again and again. Eventually, I will wake, and I will accept that Will has found the peace he so desperately sought. But today is not that day.

I wonder if he knows I am here. Witches believe in Summerland. Humans believe in Heaven. But what did Will believe in? He was neither witch nor human. Not really, anyway. Is there a place for a witch-turned-vampire-turned-human creature? And if there is, can he sense my presence from wherever he is now, wherever that place might be?

These questions, and many more, have consumed my thoughts for weeks. I never ask them aloud because we lost *her* too. While there might be a place for Will's tortured soul to rest, vampires most certainly believe there is not such a place for the undead. It would be heartless for me to search for reprieve in my comrades now that Amicia is gone. Her death is a heavy burden as well, and it tortures me so.

"I had another dream," I say softly. I stare at the ground, focusing on the murky granules of dirt that blend into mud. I sink deeper into the abyss.

Every night, in my dreams, I discover a million different ways I could have saved them. Each time, I do something differently, and that *something* is all it takes to come out heroes. I wake sooner. I fight harder. I remain stronger. I am less scared, less worried, less ... broken. I fight my grandmother's air magic, and when it no longer pins me in place, the weight is lifted from my shoulders and I am no longer frozen. I become an asset, not a hindrance, to my friends.

Since both chose to sacrifice themselves for ... *me*, I have relived that nightmare—the night they died, Will in my arms and Amicia right before my eyes—endless times. I think this is my personal hell—to live the worst moment of my life, to experience my most regretful actions, over and over again, looping round and round. Slowly, I am losing my mind to this madness, but I do not complain to the others. I deserve to be tortured by their deaths.

"This time, I morphed into some kind of superhero. Crazy costume and everything. My power was invisibility..." My mind must be grasping at straws. I lost creativity long ago—maybe on the seventh or eighth night, when I could still contemplate battle plans. Now, when I save them, I use outlandish methods, but they always seem to work. Until I open my eyes. At night, I close them, and my friends are here, with me, safe and sound. Then morning comes, and I wake. It is a cruel cycle.

Picking at a leaf that has long since dried out due to the harsh winter months, I sit back, resting my bottom on the heels of my boots. I feel the fabric of my jeans dampening from the wet cobblestone path I walked down to reach their graves. But it does not bother me. Instead, I close my eyes and listen to the sounds of nature. Before that night, Will told me to cherish the days I had, and this is the time of day when I remember to do that. During the minutes I sit with him, I pretend everything is okay.

With my eyes still closed, I pay attention to my surroundings. Winter has made way for spring. The air is warmer. The trees have buds. Early flowers bloom, spilling sweet aromas in the air. I sniffle when I think about how Will is never going to experience this again, and the fragrance tickles my nose. It smells sweet, like perfume, but I also smell Will. The pungent odor of his death is all around me, reminding me day after day that I failed him.

When bodies decay, they smell a lot like flowers. Tissue liquefies, releasing a startling sweet scent, like a bouquet of flowers that now molds and dies because I forgot to water it. By no means does it smell *good*. It just smells…different. I guess it does not smell like what I thought rotting flesh would smell like. For some reason, this brings me peace because I know part of him is still here with me. Granted, it is not the part I wanted. I would choose to keep his soul safe over his decaying body.

I open my eyes and stare at the headstones. They are perched side by side. Both are made of granite so dark they seem black, with etchings to honor those we lost. There are others beside and beyond these two because Amicia and Will are not the only vampires we lost that night, but I rarely look at the others. I never mourn their deaths. I regret their sacrifice, but I can only offer so much of my heart to the dead. Will and Amicia have consumed all that I am.

They are markers in time to remind us of what happened that night. Yes, we lost loved ones, but these tombstones are here for so many other reasons. They are meant as caution, warning us about the torment a single fruitless feud causes. They stress never again to trust the witches. Holland is our only surviving mortal ally, and it will remain that way for as long as the wounds stay fresh. I suspect we may never seek aid from a daywalker again.

The stones are arched at the top, curved and sleek, an

effortless beauty—like Amicia. They are shiny and smooth, and the parts etched with their individual names betray the lighter gray stone beneath. The small memorial cemetery is in our back garden, and the black stones blend in with the dark forest beyond the Victorian manor we call home. The moon illuminates the land, casting shadows everywhere I glance.

I stare over my shoulder. The sight of someone lurking in one of the many stained-glass windows catches my eye. But as I peer closer, squinting slightly to focus my vision on the flash of a presence, the onlooker steps away, disappearing farther into the room beyond the glass. I blink several times to clear my gaze but see no more movement.

The manor is three stories high, with startling peaks and striking overhangs. Carved embellishments true to the Victorian era are etched into the wood siding. The structure is truly a breathtaking sight.

Long ago, it was painted dark, allowing the hidden home to blend more seamlessly with its surroundings. I lived all my life in Darkhaven, yet I never knew of the manor's existence. Not until I sought refuge among the undead.

From where I sit, I can see into the kitchen, where the corner table is vacant. Just a few weeks ago, I sat at that very table with Will and discussed my future. I was torn then, unsure if I wanted to take back what the witches stole from me. Long ago, I lived a different life. That was taken from me as well. Vampirism was thrust upon me, and in a rash decision, I gave up my mortal existence in favor of immortality.

If I am honest, I was excited about the strength that came with being a vampire. I believed transitioning was the only way I could save both my life and the lives of the witches who were dying all around me. I had only seconds to make my choice, knowing I would forever live with the consequences of that day.

The doorway from the kitchen leads to a small butler's pantry, which connects to the manor's formal dining room. Again, the room is vacant. I peer through the large stained-glass windows, seeing nothing but blurry shadows from the furniture. A fire is roaring in the fireplace, and every few seconds, I hear the crackling logs from where I sit outside.

Opposite the dining room, the conservatory wraps around the entire length of the manor. I can only see the back half of the solarium, but the few wicker benches and wrought-iron table sets are home to no bodies. Perhaps there are vampires lingering in the front parlor or attached sitting room, but I doubt it. It is still early for the other vampires, with many of my housemates just now waking to greet the night.

Yes, the house is eerily silent, but that is nothing new; it has been this way for weeks. Because of Amicia's death, the vampires of this particular nest lack leadership, which they so heavily relied on before. There is a social order to vampires—a clear alpha, like a wolf pack. Now that their sire is gone, everyone is questioning every decision the hunters make.

I miss Amicia just as much as I miss Will, but I know my pain is nothing compared to the agony the vampires feel due to her absence. When a vampire is sired, a bond is formed, a connection is made. Devotion is instantaneous. But Amicia was not my sire, and even though I hate myself for feeling this way, I am grateful every single day knowing Jasik survived that battle. If I'd lost him too . . .

I shake my head, blurring the pictures that form in my mind. The sights playing on an endless loop never even happened. In my imagination, I see a different world, one where I lost everyone I cherished in one swift motion without being able to stop it. I have been torturing myself like this since that day.

Sighing loudly, I flick the dead stem from my hand, and flurries of the ripped leaf scatter before me, landing in a heap at the base of Will's headstone. That is as much as an offering as I brought with me today. Usually, I bring Will some form of a gift, be it a bundle of dried herbs or stones I gathered from the yard. But today, nothing. I suppose this is the first step to letting go.

"It is supposed to get easier," I say, but then I silently add, *but does it really? Does the pain lessen? Or as the world moves on without the departed, do we just learn to live with the agony?*

I wait, almost as though I expect an actual answer. One does not come, because Will is not here anymore to share his wisdom with me. I think of all the unanswered questions I have for him, and it pains me to know I will never know the truth. There was not enough time. I know too little about his past, about the decisions he made that led him to Darkhaven, to . . . me. Will was supposed to hold all the answers. He was supposed to be my saving grace.

Everything moves so fast here, and I forget to stop, to think, to *breathe*. I do this now, inhaling deeply through my nose and releasing that very breath through my mouth. I count to ten as I breathe in, and I hold it as long as I can before I release it again. It makes my lungs hurt to take such a long, slow breath, but the expansion of my chest smothers the pain in my heart.

I open my eyes and stare at Will's headstone.

"I think we just learn to live with the pain," I say.

I reach forward, brushing my fingertips across Will's memorial. As my fingertips tease from smooth stone to the scratchy etchings, I shiver. The sensation works its way through my arm, piercing my heart. My breathing tricks might release some of the hurt, but it never stays gone for long.

"We carry it with us, but it never gets easier," I admit. I speak so softly I am not even convinced I spoke aloud, and unfortunately, there is no one around to confirm.

I do not bother closing the door behind me as I walk into the conservatory. Nearly an hour has passed since I left to spend time outside with Will, and the other vampires of the house are finally making their way downstairs. Some are already venturing into the solarium, and then they will make their way to Amicia's gravesite. This is a daily ritual for us, and as we pass each other, no one looks up in greeting.

I stare at the ground as the others shuffle past me, and my vision remains glued to the tile floor. Vampires are all around me, and in these moments, when everyone is awake and lingering in the same part of the manor, I find it almost unbearable to live among them.

Jasik says no one blames me for what happened, but I know two deaths are at the hands of the witches—*my* witches, the very ones I fought so hard to protect. I wanted peace and prosperity, and I truly believed we could have that. I was naïve to think two utterly different creatures could remain friends.

The moment the wall transforms from drywall to sliding glass doors, I turn on my heel, entering the dining room from the solarium. The tile floor becomes hardwood, and finally, I look up, knowing I am mere steps from solitude. Those who are awake are venturing outside, so this is one of those rare moments when the kitchen should be vacant.

I maintain a schedule now around the others, keeping my distance, choosing to spend time alone or with the hunters above anyone else. Because even though no one *verbally* blames me for Amicia's death, I feel their silent accusations. I see it in their eyes, and slowly, bit by bit and day by day, their pain is smothering me.

I push open the door to the kitchen a little too forcefully, startling those who are looking for a quick meal. I choke on my breath, not expecting anyone else to be here. Shuffling to the refrigerator, I ignore my housemates, even when the itchy feeling of their gazes on my back becomes unbearable.

I grab a blood bag, noting that our supply is running dangerously low. Those who survived our last battle needed to refuel, and we ended up drinking more blood bags in one night than we drink in a month's time. Ever since then, no one has gone out to restock. I hate to think that the vampire who usually ventures into town to raid the hospital and blood banks is dead now, but that thought still crosses my mind.

I make a mental note to talk to the hunters about our supply as I close the door to the refrigerator. There is a line for the microwave, so I lean against the counter, foot tapping to a silent tune. Or maybe a countdown timer. I can never tell.

The creeping feeling of being watched makes me feel uneasy. I grow tired of waiting, so I leave the kitchen, cold blood bag in hand. I am already ripping it open with my teeth when I enter the dining room. I stop suddenly as I watch him approach.

"Ava," Malik says as an informal greeting. My trainer is still in the connected sitting room, but his long legs make it easy for him to reach my side in only a few steps.

I nod at him in greeting and begin slurping down my breakfast.

"How are you feeling?" he asks.

I lick my lips, darting my tongue at a crimson dribble that slides down the packaging. When supplies are dangerously low, I waste no blood.

I shrug in response, still not meeting his gaze, but when he clears his throat, I do. Malik is frowning at me, his eyes worrisome. Like the others, he fears my reaction to what has happened.

I think back to a conversation I had with Jasik a few days after Will's death.

"You are not handling this well," Jasik says.

"I am fine."

"I am worried about you," he replies.

I emphasized again that I was fine, even though I knew I was not. I was not prepared to admit it aloud.

"I think it is time we move on, let it go," Jasik says.

At that point, I stormed out, childlike and ornery, but I did not care. I was tired of being told to get over it. To deal with it and move on. Will deserved more respect than that. He deserved to be mourned, and I would do just that.

"It tastes better when warmed," Malik says, as if I did not already know that. Still, I am grateful for the distraction. The hunters ground me, and without them, I would never be freed from the past's clutch.

"Were you—um—*visiting* Will again?" he asks, and I do not miss his tone.

I narrow my gaze at him. I refuse to answer because he knows exactly where I was. I would not be surprised if he were the one I caught watching me earlier today.

Instead of responding, I turn on my heel, walking around him. I need to escape. When the vampires are awake, they are *everywhere*. The air becomes stifling, almost smothering. During the day, I am confined to this place, but at night, I can roam free. Of course, I never go far. I fear what would happen if I found myself closer to my former coven and farther from the vampires.

The witches are powerless, thanks to me, but I harness their magic now. Instinctively, I reach for the pendant that dangles from a thin chain around my neck. Using Will's spell, I trapped their magic in the black onyx crystal I now covet, but I fear what might happen when the magic inside calls to them—and they hear it.

I grasp the crystal in my hand, and it hums. It is a silent echo, something only I can hear. Even the vampires, with all of their heightened senses and enviable qualities, cannot feel what I feel when the magic contained inside the crystal yearns for freedom. The darkness is there too. The evil the witches created when they dabbled in black magic is confined within this gem. And it can never be released.

I hear Malik sigh heavily before walking away. I do not look back, not even when his footfalls tread lightly away. The door to the kitchen swings open, and I am alone. Finally, I relax my shoulders, dropping my arm. The pendant dangles against my skin, and I shiver.

"Ava," someone says. I hear his approach, and a shudder works its way through me. I turn to face him, and he smiles at me. It is soft and pure, his eyes shining and bright. They are crimson in color and glow bright neon red whenever he looks at me. I don't think he knows his eyes betray his deep yearning for me, but I live for it.

"Jasik," I whisper.

Suddenly, everything is better. As my sire strides toward me, looking sleepy yet beautiful at the same time, the world falls away. He is one of the few men I would call *beautiful*.

Unlike his brother, Malik, who is carved from sharp, muscular edges, Jasik is softer, leaner. Still toned, still able to change from loving to monstrous in the blink of an eye, something about Jasik speaks to me on a cellular level. I ache for him in ways I never experienced before.

He steps closer, gliding one arm behind me to pull me close, pressing firmly at the arch of my lower back. With his other arm, he tangles his fingers through my hair, which hangs in soft waves at my shoulders, until he reaches the nape of my neck. His grip is firm as he angles my head upward. The moment his lips graze mine, fireworks erupt within my chest. Jasik kisses me, softly but assuredly, and it consumes me completely. Everything slips away, leaving nothing but my innate desire for him.

When we pull away, I am smiling. Something about Jasik makes me forget the pain, the death and longing. I feel at peace, safe within his arms. In these brief moments, when we allow ourselves to relish in our purest, rawest animal instincts, time stops. It is just us, and I happily allow the world to dissipate. But he cannot press his lips against mine forever, and when I lose that connection, I am left with nothing but an endless pit, awash in despair. We can only pretend everything is okay for so long.

"Good morning," he whispers, his breath cool against my lips. He smells like mint and vanilla, like the earth and the sea all at once. He releases me, tracing his fingertips down my arms until he slides his hands against mine. We thread our fingers together, and I relish in the connection at my palms. So much of my new life is dark and lonely, empty and hollow. I need more of these moments—or I might truly lose my mind.

"Morning," I say softly. My lips are still wet with his affection, and my insides still hum from the excitement of being so close to my sire.

Our relationship has escalated since that night, and now, I guess we are an official couple. We never have any serious conversations, but with the risk of death around every corner, I almost prefer it this way. I do not want to waste time questioning my feelings. Not anymore. Not when our lives can be cut short at any moment. We are promised eternity from a hand with crossed fingers. This life is a twisted, wickedly cruel game, but it is the only one we know how to play.

I am still smiling at Jasik, staring into his eyes like a child with a schoolgirl crush, when Jeremiah tramples down the steps beside us. I glance at him, and he wiggles his eyebrows at me, his gaze darting between Jasik and me. I feel my cheeks heat and glance away.

Jasik and I have not discussed our relationship with each other, let alone the rest of the manor, so when we are caught in these moments, it almost feels like a tryst. I know our love is not forbidden—not between two creatures who seek sanctuary in the night—but it certainly feels like it is, with his being my sire and my being a former witch.

Briefly, I consider mentioning Holland, knowing Jeremiah's revitalized relationship of deepening love with the witch will surely silence the vampire, but I do not. Because secretly, my relationship with these vampires is all that is keeping me sane. When they are not around, the silence is unsettling and the shadow creeps closer.

"Look alive, people," Jeremiah says. He jumps from the final stair, landing on the floorboards beside us. The hardwood vibrates, the manor pulsating at his intrusion. "Family meeting."

I frown, glancing from Jeremiah to Jasik, who looks equally as surprised as I feel.

"Did Malik say anything to you about a meeting?" I ask.

Jasik shakes his head, and together, we walk into the parlor, plopping down on one of the sofas as we wait for the others to arrive.

"I am sure it is nothing," Jasik says.

I nod but do not respond.

"He plans to discuss our lack of sustenance," Jeremiah says, answering my earlier concerns about our dangerously low blood supply.

My fellow hunter is seated directly across from me, and though I watch him from the corner of my eye, I feign disinterest as he and Jasik continue their conversation and fears over locating more blood. Instead, I fidget with the hem of my shirt, pulling at already-loosened strings, when the slow rumble of approaching vampires creaks closer.

When I do glance up, I catch Jeremiah's steely gaze. He might be speaking to Jasik, but his attention is on me, sending a wave of irritation crashing through me. Like the others, Jeremiah is concerned. He worries about the effect our loss has had on me.

The vampires believe I am focusing too much on death, and by visiting the gravesite each night, I am welcoming agony when I should be grateful I survived. What they do not understand is focusing on Will helps me forget about everything else I lost. Amicia might not have been my sire, but she was my leader. The witches might have been awful, but they were the only family I had. Liv was my best friend. I watched my grandmother die, and I used every bit of my power to confine an ancient evil in an amulet that I now must protect. I am only seventeen. I am supposed to be thinking about boys and sneaking out to see friends, not planning funerals and protecting a town full of blissfully ignorant humans.

The sensation of being watched makes my skin prickle, and as Malik and Hikari join us in the parlor, my gaze settles on Malik, my new boss, for lack of a better term. Ever since Amicia's death, he has taken over leadership of our nest. It was not a welcomed role by any means. He would much rather hand over the reins to someone else, but there is no one. He and Jasik are the oldest vampires left, and vampires view age as strength. Malik's wisdom is supposed to protect us, and I know Amicia would have chosen him as her rightful successor if she'd had the chance.

But not everyone felt that way. We lost most of Amicia's sires after she died. They scattered, and we kept the manor. The hunters remained, vowing to protect any who wished to stay. Not many did, and now, the silence is uncanny. Day after day, I walk these empty halls, forever searching for the sounds that once made this place feel like home.

The cruelest moments are first thing in the evening, when I wake for the day, greeting the night with tired eyes. For a brief second, I forget. I do not remember the battle or Will's death. Amicia is still leader of her nest, where she belongs. The witches are still with power, and our refrigerator is stocked.

And then I blink. Then I remember.

Malik begins, his tone hard. Everything about his demeanor makes him seem far too serious for a simple family meeting, and I find myself thinking about all the years he spent by Amicia's side. The others will not admit their pain. They question my sanity because I can be hysterical and reckless, but containing such powerful emotions certainly must be more deadly than letting them loose. I might be rash, but I am still alive. Sadly, I can't say the same for all of my allies.

Malik mentions something about a local blood connection, but I am already tuning him out. My gaze flutters to the bay windows that bathe the parlor in moonlight. Outside the windows, perched atop the wraparound deck, sitting prominently at the head of the stairs, is my gargoyle.

He is dark gray in color and weather-worn from years of service. His face is scrunched in fury, the wrinkles of his face deep crevices in his otherwise smooth skin. His eyes are two lifeless dots, his ears pointed and unearthly. His teeth are bared, a clear warning to all who pass.

Not a day goes by that I do not caress his cool scalp. It has become almost ritual now. But lately, there has been animosity between us. Legend has it gargoyles are the vampires' daylight defenders. Before the witches stormed our grounds seeking nothing but death and destruction, I was naïve enough to believe the stories. I thought we were safe.

I am upset my friend did not protect us, even though I am well aware that my anger is misplaced. I should not be mad at the unworldly stone creature doomed to watch the days unfold without ever taking part in the life thriving around him, but even as I remind myself that being angry with the gargoyle is silly, I can't help the madness that washes over me.

And as my frustration grows tenfold, the amulet that hangs at my chest hums.

TWO

I know I am dreaming. The feeling of my body asleep, heavy and unyielding, on my bed in the manor is as clear as the sunny day around me. My lungs are full and heavy with each inhalation. The sunlight against my skin is warm, comforting—something I have not experienced in quite a long time.

Despite knowing I am asleep, this place is no less real to me. In my mind, I am here—with him—and we are safe. It always happens like this, which is why it is becoming increasingly difficult to discern fantasy from reality, imagination from vision.

Jasik smiles at me, but he looks so different from the vampire I know. His eyes are bright, his irises a sparkling blue. His skin is tan and smooth, and I reach out to touch it, letting my hand graze the muscular edges of his body. Everything about him is familiar—from the way his body presses against mine to the way he touches me—even if his appearance plays tricks on me.

His lips never move, yet he tells me how happy he is. I feel it too. That moment of peace. But lurking at the edges of our picturesque life is darkness. It creeps closer, bleeding into the frame. With spider web veins, it seeps in, surrounding us, clinging to my skin.

I blink and everything changes. I see it in his eyes—he

recognizes it too. The evil presence is all around us, smothering, basking in our happiness.

The sun above us is suddenly obstructed. I have to shield my gaze to look at it, and I watch as something dark and sinister covers what was once bright and glowing. The eclipse shrouds the earth in gloom, and I can do nothing to stop what is already here.

The world is cloaked in shadow, and I feel its presence in my bones. I shiver as Jasik's eyes turn from a cool, light aqua to a stark, glowing crimson. The vampire surfaces, emerging as it senses danger.

My sire cools under my touch, and I jerk away from him as if he has lashed out at me. I don't mean to react the way I do, but something revolting washes over me—something eerie and sinister is in our midst. My senses are rapid firing, warning me of danger at all sides.

The shadows loom closer, and I feel them. They are thick, stagnant in the air, and when they touch me, I cringe.

And then it happens. Somehow, I expect it. I have had this nightmare over and over again ever since I returned to this place. It's always different yet still the same. I anticipate his death, but the pain still envelopes me in a fury I have never known.

Awash with grief, I watch as my lover's hard curves become soft, like whispers against untouched skin. He bursts into ash. I blink, and he is gone, whisked away with the breeze, forever out of grasp. I clutch my chest as the pain creases, my heart imploding at the sight of losing Jasik.

I am alone now, and with each exhalation, I see my breath. My lip quivers and I hold myself, cradling my torso beneath my arms. I scratch at them with my nails, desperate to ground myself. I fear I may float away, forever spinning out of control in this obsidian abyss that surrounds me.

The air becomes heavy with smoke. I squint through the haze, but the mist intensifies. My lungs burn, and I choke on my breath. My fear intensifies, and I scream. But the noise that I emit sounds nothing like me. I do not recognize the lost, helpless girl who weeps, even though she wears my face.

I clutch at my throat, scratching the skin raw. I know this will not help; this will not send oxygen rushing into my lungs any faster. In fact, this is making it harder to breathe, and even though I am aware of this, I cannot stop. I claw, viciously, like a predator tearing through prey.

I wince as my nails dig into flesh, scraping the area bloody. I crumble, falling to my knees. My body slams against the cold, frozen tundra, and a sharp cramp shoots through my thighs, burrowing itself deep into the base of my spine. I feel the pain everywhere, all at once, and I shriek, silently, because even though I gasp for air, I cannot breathe.

As I slowly drift into unconsciousness, a cackle resonates all around me. The faster I die, the louder it becomes.

I jolt awake, drenched in sweat. Sitting upright and breathing heavily, I run a hand through my damp hair, tangling what is already a heaping mess. With sleepy eyes, I glance at Jasik, who still slumbers beside me. I watch as his chest rises and falls with each inhalation.

Seeing him breathe—how simple it seems—calms my racing heart. Before long, the dizzy haze of my dream dissipates, and I quickly forget the pain and the fear that comes with my nightmares.

I dangle my legs over the side of the bed, planting my feet firmly against the hardwood floors. I slouch forward, resting my elbows on my thighs and forehead against my palms. I close my eyes and exhale sharply, gnawing on my lower lip. The worst part about sleeping isn't the inevitable nightmares that follow—it's *talking* about them the next day. So if I don't wake Jasik, I don't tell him about them. It just seems easier that way.

After drowning in self-pity, I stand and tiptoe toward the bathroom, glancing back at our bed only once I have crossed the threshold. Confident I haven't woken my sire, I close the door and slump forward, allowing my palms to linger against the cool wood once it is firmly shut. Again, I close my eyes, preferring the darkness of my mind over the reality of my visions. I remain like this until the hammering in my head ceases.

By the time I step away and look at myself in the mirror, I am confident I can forget about my dream. Sometimes, what I conjure while I sleep haunts me throughout the day. Other times, I am able to remain blissfully unaware of what may come.

It may be careless to write off this one as just another nightmare, especially considering my affinity for spirit, but these warnings come too often to properly vet. The more frequently I have them, the harder it is to sense whether or not they are foreboding visions or the result of an overactive imagination. So I have decided to ignore them and let fate define our path. Our greatest enemy—the witches—is no longer a threat, and I am confident we can best anyone else who brings trouble our way.

Still, I am shaken by them. Watching Jasik die again and again is not helping my sanity. It isn't helping our relationship either. I feel myself pulling away from him. The thought of losing him hurts so much, I almost wonder if it will be easier if I weren't so . . . invested. I hate myself for even thinking this, but I've lost so much. I can't bear the thought of losing my sire too.

I turn on the tap and splash water on my face. I let the droplets drip onto the countertop, and I stare as they pool before me, molding into shapes that look eerily similar to the monsters from my favorite children's stories. I used to read them under the covers at bedtime with nothing but a flashlight guiding my way.

I hold out my hand and concentrate, summoning an element to dry the mess I've made. The air shifts slightly. It tingles and vibrates against my exposed skin. The pooled water ripples before blowing into the sink, disappearing down the drain.

I complete my task easily, even though I rarely rely on my magic these days.

I admit I have been in a rut. Living with the vampires has almost suppressed my magical half—just like the dark spell. They don't ask me to keep from casting spells, but after everything the witches did, it feels strange to harness magic in this house and around my nestmates. They harbor no ill will toward me for what the witches did, but I still bear the weight of it. It compresses against my chest, forcing the pounding beats of my overworked heart into my head until I can hear nothing else. It is a constant reminder of what they did, of what we lost.

I finish my morning routine and change into new clothes. Before I exit my bedroom, I glance over my shoulder one last time. Jasik still sleeps. Knowing he—and the rest of the house—won't rise for at least another hour, I close the door behind me.

I crouch beside his headstone, brushing off the debris that fell overnight. The stone is rough against my palm, and it sends a shiver down my spine. Everything about this place feels cold, yet I visit it, day after day. I tell myself Will is not here. None of them are, but that does not ease the pain.

"I miss you," I say. The stone stares back at me, blank and mute. This place is cold and lifeless—so different from the warmth of skin or the glint of a devious glare. Nothing about this place represents the souls lost that day.

I feel it as I do every time I come here. The anger rises in my chest, leaving a bitter taste in my mouth.

I hate the witches for what they did, and I am ashamed that I was born from their blood.

I hate this evil entity that I must now protect. It does not deserve my protection or my allegiance, but if it falls into the hands of someone with evil intentions...

I sigh and shake away the thought, balling my hands into fists at my sides. I bury my fingernails into my flesh, easing the pressure only when I feel the familiar bite of broken skin. It heals quickly, and I am suddenly consumed by my guilt.

My comrades relied on my protection, my aid, and even though I am swarming with power, I could not save them. And I cannot bring them back. I rely on my magic to heal unnecessary wounds while Will decomposes, buried deep in the earth. Nothing about this is fair.

I sink lower, resting my bottom on my heels. For only a moment, I allow my anger to rise in my chest until I feel nothing but the burning, formidable desire to bring this entire town to its knees. I want to avenge our fallen. I want the witches to pay the ultimate price—like my friends paid. I want them to answer for their mistakes, and I want the cost to be more than relinquishing their magic. That isn't enough. That will *never* be enough.

Once I am seething, trembling so violently I can barely contain my rage, I allow myself the gift of forgiveness. I release the hate, refusing to allow it to corrode my innards. In one sweeping burst, it escapes me, and the ground shakes. The earth responds to my longing in a way the witches never could. It weeps with me, quivering right to its very core.

My skin is hot, sticky, and I swipe at the sweat that beads at my temple. My magic explodes from my body, and the sudden change in temperature has caused a mist to form. The air thickens and fogs, making it difficult to breathe, but I try to ignore these signs.

I remember my dream, my fear, my pain—and I let it all go. Hunching forward, I weep. I release the elements, and I cry until the tears refuse to flow. My eyes burn as I wipe away that which is not there. I press hard, involuntarily so, almost as if I am *trying* to force more tears. But none come.

I want to tell Will that it is not fair, that he should never have been the sacrifice in this war. He deserved to survive, to leave this place and create the life he always dreamed of having. The good should not be the cost of peace. But I can't bring myself to admit these things, even though this stone has heard them all before. I try not to think about all the times I have promised to avenge his death, because I have lost count.

During my darkest moment, I even fancied the idea of bringing him back, of dabbling in the dark arts and summoning an entity so evil and so powerful it could raise the dead. But I never did. And I never will. Not because I don't want to and not because I can't access such magic. I know I can. I know this power exists if only I just tap into it.

The reason I don't is *because* of Will. I would need to succumb to the most sinister parts of my soul, and I couldn't bear the way he would look at me when he discovered the truth. He would hate me forever, and I am ashamed to admit that the only thing worse than losing him would be knowing he's alive and has no desire to see me.

So instead of more broken promises, I say, "I hope you're proud of me."

But I don't know why I say this. I have done nothing to deserve Will's pride. He died while saving me, offering his life in an effort to save the rest of us. He was a better, kinder, stronger, smarter soul than any of us. We didn't deserve his loyalty.

"I'm sorry," I whisper, my voice breaking. "I'm sorry I couldn't save you."

And then I hear it. Cackling from somewhere above me, as though the creature from my nightmare mocks my words. My blood runs cold as I flash back to that moment in my dream, when the sound erupted from the depths of darkness, surrounding me, smothering me.

I look up and see it. Perched on the highest part of a nearby tree, a crow watches me. My breath catches as I stare back at it, and I feel my pulse race. I become lightheaded, but I cannot look away. Frozen in place, my eyes dry at the bitterly cold morning air. Tears burn, but I still do not blink, not until I am certain I am *really* seeing what I think is there.

Because this must be a dream. It has to be. Am I still asleep? Again, I dig my nails into my palms and wince at the pain. But I do not wake.

I remember my training. *Mamá* was clear in our lessons. Crows are evil. They are the bringers of death and malice. I am certain this is an omen. A warning. A *threat*.

I stand abruptly and make the quick decision to scare the bird from our property. I shout and wave my arm at it, but it does not budge. Instead, slowly, it crooks its head, allowing me to see its stark profile against the moonlit sky. Its beak is long and sharp, and it cackles again.

The bird is watching me. Its beady, gleaming eye glistens in the starlight, and even though I know it is not possible, I am certain it is smiling at me. As if it knows something I do not.

Jasik treads down the stairs just as I am walking into the sitting room. The sight of him still leaves me breathless sometimes— even though I am still trying to calm down after my encounter with the crow. I am feeling dizzy and lightheaded, and my heart is beating so hard I am certain my sire hears it.

He frowns when he sees me, and I wonder if I am flushed. I swipe at my forehead, finding it dewy. I imagine my cheeks are about three shades redder than usual, and from the look of concern etched across his face, Jasik knows something is amiss. As much as I strive to conceal these parts of myself from him, I know I won't be able to keep these secrets for long.

"Ava? Is everything okay?" he asks as he strides toward me.

He closes the space between us in a couple of easy steps. Before I know it, he is before me. He reaches forward, gliding his fingertips along the curve of my jaw, tipping my head back so our gazes lock. I push away his hand, not wanting my eyes to betray my inner turmoil before I am ready.

"What is it?" he asks, his voice wavering. He grows more confused—frightened even—with each second I do not respond.

I shake my head, a desperate attempt to convince myself what I saw was nothing more than coincidence. All of these things—my dreams, my innate fear, the crow—could be chalked up to an overactive imagination. They could also be the product of the turmoil we experienced not so long ago. Our anxiety is heightened, so it makes sense that I am not feeling like myself. If I label them as deviant, then the threat I might be foreseeing becomes real. It exists, and it is a force to be reckoned with.

And I'm not sure that will help our situation. The vampires put on a brave face, but we are still broken. The few weeks that have passed since I hexed the witches were not enough to mend our fractured souls, and this certainly hasn't been enough time to wage war on yet another enemy.

"Ava . . . " Jasik says, voice stern. My sire is making it clear that he will not let this go. Even though I crave silence, I can't keep pushing him away. The flicker inside me that tethers our souls together won't allow it either. Our bond might not grant him total control over me, but it's enough to make me *want* to please him.

"It's nothing," I admit. "I was in the cemetery. I saw . . . " I hesitate.

The significance of crows is important in witchcraft, so I doubt Jasik will understand. He might brush off this as nothing more than migrating birds. While that might seem ideal, I am conflicted. I'm not sure what's worse—keeping the vampires in the dark or exposing them to my other side and watching as they dismiss my witchy concerns.

"What did you see? Is this about your nightmare?" he asks, breaking my silence.

I suck in a sharp breath. So I did wake him. He does know. I swallow hard, shaking my head. Even as I deny the connection between my dreams and the crow stalking us outside, something within me stirs. The part of me who was raised in a coven knows better. The spirit witch is certain the two are connected, even if I can't quite speak it aloud.

"There was a crow," I blurt. "Perched on one of the tree branches. It was *watching* me. I'm sure of it."

Jasik frowns, pauses, and I think he is considering his words before responding. Maybe I was wrong about him. After all, he has never doubted me before. So why now? I fear my insecurities are getting the best of me. Ever since we lost Will and the others, I have lost my faith, and the emptiness inside me has filled with resentment and uncertainty. I need to find my strength, and my faith, if there truly is danger afoot.

"Are crows significant?" he asks.

I nod.

"What do they mean?"

"Crows can cross between the spiritual and physical world. They carry souls over to the other side after death," I explain.

"That doesn't necessarily sound strange," Jasik says. "We just experienced . . . *casualties*." I do not miss his hesitation or how he emphasizes casualties as if it physically *hurt* him to speak the word aloud. Knowing the pain he is hiding, my chest burns for him.

"Crows are *not* good omens," I say, speaking slowly, firmly. "These birds are tricksters by nature."

"Okay," Jasik says, nodding, thinking. He meets my gaze. "So what do we do?"

I shake my head. "There's nothing we can do except prepare for the inevitable."

"And what is that?" he asks.

Just as I am about to explain how bad things might get, especially if both my dreams and the crows are meant as warnings, Jeremiah and Holland descend the stairs and step into the sitting room. Although we are in the same room, Jasik and I are standing closer to the entrance to the conservatory, so a small part of me hopes they don't notice us. The last thing I need right now is to explain my dreams—the ones where I watch Jasik die, night after night, in a million different horrible ways—to the rest of our nest.

Holding hands and smiling, the two lovers laugh, paying us no attention, as if they are the only two beings left in existence. I welcome this invisibility, but it does not last long. As soon as I acknowledge it in my mind, it dissipates and we are seen.

"Morning!" Holland cheers when he finally sees us.

I nod at him and avert my gaze, settling on the floor. My eyes will betray every conflicted emotion circling around my mind, and I am not ready for him to see them. At least not yet. Not until after I tell Jasik about my dreams.

"Uh-oh," Jeremiah says. "I know that look."

I dare a peek, relieved to find him staring at Jasik, not me. My relief is short-lived because I make the mistake of glancing at Holland, who drops Jeremiah's hand and shuffles over to me.

"What is it?" Holland asks. "What's happened?"

"Ava is seeing crows," Jasik says.

The color leaves Holland's face, and I swallow the knot

that forms in my throat. I thought I could convince myself that there is nothing to worry about, that this was only a coincidence. But the look of absolute terror strewn across Holland's face tells me I was reckless and stupid for holding on to such childish dreams.

I don't live in a world of light anymore. I reside in darkness, where the monsters lurking threaten every aspect of my new life. I should have known they would come for Jasik. I was ill-prepared before. Now, I must ready myself for war because I will protect my sire at all costs.

"What does that mean?" Jeremiah asks. He looks from Jasik to Holland to me, becoming increasingly puzzled because no one speaks. It occurs to me that Jeremiah knows very little about witchcraft, which is strange considering he dates a witch.

"It's a very bad omen," Holland whispers. He stares at me curiously, and I assume he is wondering why I kept this from him, from everyone. As a spirit user, I should have seen this coming long before crows showed up. And I did. I just ignored the signs.

"How bad are we talking?" Jeremiah asks, utterly blind to the internal conversation I am having with Holland as I use my eyes to beg for his forgiveness.

"Crows are bringers of death," I say, defeated. I know hiding this from them wasn't my smartest decision, but can they blame me for expecting peace after everything we have been through?

"What does that even mean?" Jeremiah asks. "Are you telling me I need to be scared of a bird?" He doesn't bother hiding his humor in the idea of a vampire fearing an animal. After all, we are supposed to be at the top of the food chain.

Very little should frighten us.

Holland sighs heavily, clearly irritated by his boyfriend's bluntness, and I am beginning to understand why their relationship did not last the first time around. That only saddens me now. After so much loss, we need a little love in our lives.

"Yes," I say, hoping to save Holland from being the one to answer Jeremiah. "Be afraid because crows are only the *first* sign. Something sinister always follows."

"Something sinister? Like what?" Jeremiah asks, crossing his arms over his chest.

"What should we look for?" Jasik asks, ignoring his ally and directing his question to me.

Something flashes between us, and in my mind's eye, I see my dream unfold. Jasik may be standing before me perfectly healthy, perfectly safe, completely fine, but he is also bursting into flames, his ash blowing away before I even realize he is gone.

How can I tell him this? If my nightmares were visions of what is to come, then how can I reveal his future? How am I supposed to explain my sire's days are numbered? The clock is ticking steadily down, and the approaching buzzer rings all around me, even now, even when I know he is okay.

There is a reason I haven't confessed my nightmares to him. Beneath all of this inherent strength, I am truly weak, and the thought of losing yet another friend fills me with an anguish I have never before experienced. I would give up all that I have, every power at my disposal, if only I could guarantee we would finally be safe.

"That all depends on what is coming," Holland cuts in.

I glance over, silently thanking him for rescuing me

after my lips fall numb.

"Do you have any idea what that might be?" Jasik asks me. His gaze is still fixed on me. My sire is ever persistent, and I know he will not accept silence. Now is the time.

I gnaw on my lower lip, knowing this is it. This is the moment I must confess, spilling all my dirty secrets about my nightmares and what happens within them. I just wish I didn't have to reveal what might be Jasik's death while standing in front of the others. While it might not be my right to keep his destiny a secret, it is his. If I told him the first time I saw him die in my dreams, everything might be different now. He might understand my desire for make-believe.

"Crows are not the worst of it," I admit, allowing the shame to coat my words.

"What do you mean?" Jasik asks.

While my voice breaks and squeaks at the most inopportune time, his is strong, unwavering in his interrogation of my ulterior motives.

I exhale slowly, building my resolve. Finally, when I feel brave enough to admit what I have seen, I open my mouth to speak, knowing the words are now eager to spill from me, but I am silenced. I am stopped just when I am prepared to detail every horrific dream, every lived nightmare, because the front door crashes open. I hear the stained-glass windows' protest—the ear-piercing splinter of glass nearly shattering upon impact pulsates through me.

We all jerk toward the door, unsure of what is to come. All prepared for what may be our darkest moment, I watch as Holland readies himself to call upon his magic to aid Jeremiah, even as Jeremiah sidesteps to block his lover from what may be an attacker.

We release the tension in our bodies as Malik stomps into the sitting room and halts when he sees us. Dressed in combat attire, he was clearly patrolling the forest surrounding the manor, a nightly ritual we all sign up for—even our newly elected leader. After spending the last several months hunting these very woods, I know returning home so soon can only mean one thing: he found something.

"What is it?" Jasik asks. "What happened?" He steps forward, inching closer to Malik, who is clearly shaken by whatever is happening outside the manor.

Not usually one to showcase such visible emotions, Malik clenches his jaw, his body growing rigid as Jasik continues to step forward.

Releasing a long, slow breath, Malik glances at me, and I freeze. I see it in his eyes. It's there—something dark, something dangerous.

Does he know?

Holland peers back at me, anxiety muddling his normally bright eyes, but I ignore him. I don't need to look at him to know what he is thinking. Whatever spirit tried to warn me about is here—in Darkhaven. It has begun, and based on Malik's reaction, whatever it is likely has everything to do with me. And my silence over the past several weeks.

Outside, the wind howls. The transition between seasons is never friendly to this part of the world. Winter is making way for spring, but it is not relenting without a fight.

An icy blast of air bellows through the foyer, where the front door has been left open. I shiver, even though I do not experience the cold the way I once did. It does not threaten my life the way it does a mortal, but I am aware of its presence, like a thick cloak hanging over me. That isn't all that is there, though. Something else lingers in the darkness, and it is close—even now.

Malik still has not answered Jasik's question, and it is obvious he doesn't intend to. He waits, but as the silence stretches on, the seconds seem to last a lifetime.

"Malik—"

Jasik stops. In unison, we suck in a sharp breath. All at once, we are aware. We sense it. We smell it. We feel it looming ever closer, nearing the manor with precision, as if it has been coming for us all along.

I release my breath first, only to gulp down another just as quickly. I have loathed this very scent ever since it first emerged in my dreams. Overshadowing my better judgment, I say aloud what we all know to be true.

"It's smoke," I confess. "Darkhaven is on fire."

But my sudden rush of fear for the unsuspecting humans of my small town is overridden by my dread for my lover. Because only I know that this fire is meant not for the people of Darkhaven but for us.

For me.

For him.

THREE

My feet pound against the earth, the vibration of its vicious beating resonating through my legs. It soothes my nervous muscles—the very ones I have not used in battle for far too long.

I feel the call to war like a wolf feels the pull of the moon. I have come to understand that chaos is in my blood, and the reality of that makes the crystal dangling at my neck buzz with excitement. I smile as it warms against my skin. In these moments of turmoil, it sparks to life, reminding me that it is only one magical burst away from aiding me if I should ever need its assistance.

As Jasik, Malik, and I swiftly approach the village of Darkhaven, my heart is ready for this fight, but my mind is elsewhere. I replay my conversation with the other hunters over and over again, a sickening, twisted way to continue torturing myself.

Holland has never been one to brawl. Even though Amicia always considered him an invaluable asset and strong ally, his time is better spent in the books and cooking up spells. He despises confrontation—I know that now. And the more I think about how often I have brought this feud directly to him, the more my insides twist into a painful lump. I hate myself for getting him involved, even if his arrival meant the reconciliation of his romance with Jeremiah.

Jeremiah and Hikari are not with us either. With Holland offering to stay behind to protect the manor and remaining vampires in case our assumption is correct—that this fire proves to be a trap—Jeremiah made it clear he was staying behind too.

We all agreed we might be walking into a bad situation, but only Jeremiah feared the trap might not be for those who go but for those who stay behind. And with that dreadful thought consuming his imagination, he refused to leave Holland behind. I admire his loyalty to his partner, and I can't blame him for ditching us in favor of love.

Hikari said she was staying behind to help ease Jeremiah's guilt for choosing Holland over his duties, and no one argued, even though we are all secretly aware that the loss of Amicia has taken a great toll on her. The truth is, ever since we lost our leader, Hikari has been...different. She mopes silently through the house, keeping her head down and her nose out of our troubles.

I could tell Malik was contemplating ordering her to join us, but he never did. We didn't argue with her logic, because in the end, we are a group of six. Splitting us down the middle, divvying our strength so everyone has a fair chance, seemed like the right thing to do. But was it the *smart* thing? I guess we will find out.

Thinking about our situation gives me a headache. It took mere seconds to make our decision to aid Darkhaven, but in doing so, we were forced to abandon both the manor and remaining vampires who call it home. Before, rushing to help another came easy to us, but now, without Amicia, we have to choose—the manor and the vampires who rely on our protection, or Darkhaven. Should the decision come so easily?

The closer I am to the billowing smoke, the more I start to wonder if running toward a blazing inferno with only two allies beside me is a good idea. After all, Darkhaven still has witches to protect it. My nest only has five hunters and a witch who despises conflict.

As we approach the edge of the forest, I clear my mind, readying myself for what may wait beyond the tree line. There is no point in hashing out past mistakes when I can't change them—and honestly, I don't even know how I *would* change them. Both our vampires and the humans need protection. But what's done is done. I need to remain focused and diligent if I am to overcome the mess we're in.

With smoke swirling upward into the dark sky, I realize even the moon is hiding, as if it too fears what is to come. The uneasiness settles over me, like a warm blanket on a hot day. It makes my skin crawl, and I fight the urge to scratch at my flesh.

Something flashes in the darkness, and I almost welcome the distraction. I peer toward the treetops to get a better look, all while effortlessly maneuvering through brush.

At first, I discover nothing but darkness, each shadow forming its own shape. As I rush steadfast into the unknown, the shadows morph into something else completely. And then I see it—at least, I think I do. Something dark and menacing, watching and waiting. I think it smiles at me, but I know that's impossible, for crows cannot smile. The glint in its beady eye drains the blood from my body, and I nearly pass out.

I come to an abrupt stop and rest my palm against a nearby tree. The bark is rough, and it scratches my palm. I welcome the sensation, letting it ground me as I continue to stare at the bird. While I catch my breath, I clutch my chest, but my fingers are drawn to the crystal. I squeeze it tightly, finding the stark edges of stone comforting.

"Ava, what is it?" Jasik asks. He speaks slowly, carefully, and I'm sure the sight of me holding the amulet is revolting, considering what this weapon contains. But I don't release it. It almost feels like I *can't*. Like the pendant itself refuses to relinquish *me*, not the other way around.

Jasik's gaze follows mine, trailing upward. He squints, allowing his vision to adjust to the darkness looming overhead. I know the exact moment he sees it. He sucks in a sharp breath and holds it, and that's when I know the crow isn't my imagination playing tricks on me. It is really there. Watching. Waiting. It caws, a forceful burst that makes me flinch, and I know it's warning me of impending doom.

"Is that—"

"The crow," I whisper, cutting him off.

"Let's go. We need to keep moving," Malik says. He never looks up.

A natural-born leader, Malik is always the voice of reason during even my darkest moments, and even though I want to obey, I can't. My legs do not move. My limbs are numb and heavy, and my vision swirls. My mind races with the realization of what is happening. Holland and I were right to fear the crow, for it brings nothing but devastation.

"I know what it is warning us about," I say, my voice so low I wonder if I have even spoken at all.

"What? What is it? What's coming?" Jasik asks. His brow furrows, forming a deep crease.

"The fire," I whisper. "The witches."

We emerge through the tree line and step onto the property of my childhood home. It looms overhead, boxy in shape, with startling gray wood planks weather-worn by the tumultuous winter months.

The woods spill into the backyard, and I think about all the times I played here as a child. I never had that fancy playground equipment my other friends had in their backyards, but I never needed that. Even as a child, spirit was strong. I would invoke the elements, garnering just a taste before my strength dwindled.

I close my eyes and see it: me, as a child, wrapping sticks in twine to create villagers. I would craft their homes out of stones I found littering the streets. I buried bricks, leaving only the tops bare, to form roads. My little village resembled Darkhaven, a place I loved calling home. Now, the sight of it makes me sick.

I walk closer, the shock of what I see silencing my cries. The stump in the center of the yard that is used as their altar during rituals was from a tree that fell after a particularly gruesome storm. My father repurposed it, and it remained there ever since. I remember watching him prepare nature's offering. *Abuela* was by his side, using her air magic to slice through the trunk with such ferocity and precision, I ran back inside the house and refused to come out.

That was my first real taste of the power behind magic and the first time I feared my elders. Afterward, I made a point of obeying any order, of becoming the best witch I could possibly be—even if my coven's constant doubt in my abilities made it difficult to remain obedient.

I am reminded of all these things because as I walk through the backyard, wavering closer to the house I lived in all my life, I am mute. I can't speak my truth aloud, but I relive these memories in my mind. They loop round and round, smothering what little optimism I have.

The fumes are so strong I can hardly breathe. The house my father built with his own two hands is on fire, the thick smoke swirling into the air, black and ominous.

In the distance, I hear the crow's caw. It morphs from an eerie, singsong melody to a harsh, abrupt caw, as if its life has been smothered too.

"Ava," Jasik says softly.

His voice pleads with me, as though he is afraid of what I might do. But what can I do? The damage has been done. I cannot save my house, but the people inside . . . My *mother* . . . I have to believe she made it out. A strong spirit witch has the ability to tap into the elements—any one of which could have saved her.

Something prickles in the back of my mind. Something I know I am supposed to remember. But every time I search my memory to unveil the secrets there, the crystal at my chest burns against my skin. I wince at the pain, even as I welcome the distraction.

I step closer, ignoring the voices of reason behind me. Drowned out by the thickness of the air, my allies are suppressed. I cough and blink excessively, but my eyes still sting; my lungs still ache. And my feet continue moving forward, as if I am no longer in control, driven by a force I cannot see.

"We can't go inside," someone shouts. I think it's Malik, but I am not sure.

I am only a few feet away from the sliding glass doors that once led to the dining area off the kitchen. The glass is gone, shattered and scattered across the grass. It crunches beneath my feet, burrowing deeply into the soles of my boots. Somehow, I know they will remain lodged there, even if I try to dig them out. A small piece of the beauty this house once embodied, they will remain with me for years to come.

Something occurs to me. What if my mother is trapped upstairs? It's late. She should have been asleep when the fire was cast. I glance up, moving my arm to shield my eyes from the bright orange flames that lick the side of the house. The fire is warm and radiant as I try to locate the bedroom windows. They too are gone. Flames flutter through the open squares, dancing to silent music heard only in my mind. It is a sickening song, but I sway to it as I try to steady my footing.

Someone grabs my arm. I feel the firmness of his grasp, and I turn to face him. The vision of Jasik is blurred before me, and this is when I realize I am crying. I did not feel the tears, even though I am engulfed in the pain. I collapse against him, erupting in anguish and anger. I scream against his chest, but his solid, muscular frame swallows the sound—almost as if I never made a noise.

"We need to leave," Malik says, and I feel Jasik's body jostle as he nods in agreement.

The exact moment I want to argue against leaving, I remember what the intensity of this fire made me forget. The crystal at my neck cools as I remember, and I grab on to it, making certain it is still there. The sudden flash of truth—that this crystal *made* me forget this horror—floods me with fear.

"Let's go, Ava," Malik says when I don't move.

But I can't leave. Don't they understand? I can barely move. I am rooted in place, secured by the realization that *I did this*. I might not have struck the match that lit the flame, but I left them powerless. As much as I hate my former coven for the hell they put me through, I would never have condemned them to this, to being burned alive. The irony overwhelms me, igniting my own internal blaze.

I push Jasik away, stumbling backward. As they approach, I shout at them to stay away from me. They think I am upset with them. I can see the pain and confusion strewn across their faces, but that's not why I need space. I'm afraid that if they get too close, I'll hurt them. Not because I want to. Because I *have* to. The sensation to commit an evil act is bubbling inside me, fueled by the fire encircling us.

I ball my hands into fists at my sides, squeezing so hard I am certain I will crush the tiny bones there. I dig my nails into my palms until I bleed, and I let the smell of my own blood wash over me. The sound of my grumbling stomach calms me, helping to steady my breath. Focusing on just one sense, when they are all rapid firing, helps to clear my mind.

But I am still angry. Only now, my anger has turned to hunger. I crave answers in a way I have never before experienced, and I know I will discover the truth, even if I have to let this whole town burn in order to find it.

"Ava, we must leave," Malik says. "Humans are already starting to gather out front. I can hear them. Focus on that sound. Let it ground you."

He holds his arms out before him as if to caution me. His eyes are wide, but the loud beat of his heart echoes in my mind. He is afraid. But why? Is he afraid of me or of what I plan to do?

"Listen to them," he says again.

I nod, and taking his advice, I listen. My senses stretch out around me, cascading through the house until I reach the front door.

And that's when I hear it.

A dozen tiny voices screaming for help.

The witches.

I suck in a sharp breath, my eyelids jolting open.

Something flashes behind Jasik's eyes—maybe fear or the desire to stop me—but I am gone before he can protest. I sprint into the house. I make it to the front door, steering to the right to take the stairs two at a time.

Halfway up the creaky stairs, I slam my foot too hard against wavering wood, and my leg falls through. I drop down, catching myself before my entire body plummets into the embers beneath. Still, the flames dance across my boot, and my feet swell and sweat at the intense heat ravishing below. As I try to gain better footing to free myself, I wiggle my moist toes. Sweat dribbles down my forehead as I pull myself up, grunting so loudly I am shocked the others don't come to my aid.

Out of breath and dizzy from hunger, I crawl up the rest of the stairs until I reach the top landing.

Standing tall, I swipe away the sticky sweat at my temples and stumble forward. My boot and jeans are singed, exposing the burnt flesh beneath. It is raw and bruised, and I grind my teeth as I carry on, ignoring the stabbing pain in my calf, knowing it will eventually heal on its own. But my mother won't be so lucky.

I open my bedroom door, finding no one, but still, I whimper as I watch the few belongings I once possessed perish in the fire. I leave it open and limp to the guest room door—again, I find it empty.

I hobble to my mother's room and reach for the knob. I suck in a sharp breath and yank my hand free. The emblem on the doorknob is burned into my flesh, so I ball my fist and bang on the door, screaming for my mother. No one responds.

I step to the side, resting my palms against the warm wood walls, and use my good leg to kick open the door. A blast of flames erupts into the hallway, and I stumble backward, just out of reach. I throw my arms up in defense, summoning enough air magic to steer the blaze away from me. It bursts from my palms, shooting as cascading puffs of icy wind. It quickly smothers the flames meant to tarnish my flesh.

Weakened, I crawl to the door, the heat within the bedroom so intense I can barely keep my eyes open.

Peering into her room, I whisper her name. No one responds. I call louder, my chest heaving, gasping for breath. Still, I receive no response. My gaze settles on her bed, which is doused in fire. But she is not there.

With every room cleared, I claw my way to the stairs. I pull myself up using the railing, and when I place my foot on the first step, the floor crumbles beneath me. I teeter, nearly falling into the fiery abyss, but I manage to maintain my hold on the rail long enough to leap down.

I land awkwardly, and something in my ankle snaps. I shriek and stumble forward, landing on my behind. I lean against the front door, grabbing hold of my ankle as I close my eyes, my head spinning. I curse inwardly, the pain almost too much to bear.

Already my bones are mending, using my heightened vampire abilities to heal the torn flesh. But I try not to focus on my wounds. I will survive this fire, but I know others won't be as lucky. I listen for the voices I heard earlier—except now, I can only hear my vampire allies. Jasik and Malik are arguing outside.

"We have to help her!" Jasik shouts.

"Stop!" Malik shouts. "You are blinded by your feelings for her."

Jasik pleads with his brother to release him, and I know Malik must have bested him in a fight. They continue to argue, and I know Malik will never release him. The only thing he fears more than losing his hunters is losing his little brother.

"Look at the house, Jasik," Malik says. "Entering is suicide."

At that, I open my eyes. All around me, the fire flashes, sizzling and luminescent. With each second I remain seated at the front entrance, the heat intensifies. I feel it lick my skin, and I wonder if I will melt before I find the witches. Malik is right, this is certain death.

Just when I allow his warning to get the best of me, I hear them again. The timing is so perfect, I wonder if the gods and goddesses truly *want* me to save them.

They whimper, their voices weak. And all at once, I know where they are.

I lunge forward, limping through the hallway as my ankle continues to heal. I move as quickly as I can, seething with each step I take. I reach the closet door, thrusting it open so harshly it breaks from its hinge. I push it aside and step through.

The basement door is already ajar, and thick wafts of smoke seep through the small opening. I pull it open enough to squeeze through, and I cover my mouth with my arm as the smog intensifies. As I descend into the flashing pit, this does nothing to help my breathing, so I continue to hack, peering only through slits in my eyelids.

I reach the bottom step and lean against the wall. I gasp, sucking in a long lungful of air but feeling no closer to actually breathing. I am woozy from blood loss, giddy from lack of oxygen, and groggy from hunger, and somehow, I know I won't make it out of this basement without help. It's a stark realization that washes over me, clinging to my chest, pressing down on what little lung capacity I have maintained during this daring rescue.

As I search for my former comrades, I come to another reality.

The basement is empty.

But that can't be. I *know* I heard them. I felt their pain, listened to their cries for help. It wasn't my imagination, I am sure of it. And yet, I am alone, greeted only by the everlasting flames, which seem to grow deadlier with each passing second.

I am trapped. Alone. Surrounded by nothing but a crackling, hungry fire. I sense the way it craves my body, my life—I have felt that similar desperate desire rooted so deeply I could obey nothing else beyond my blood lust. I know I am not safe. It will stop at nothing to claim my soul.

I press firmly against the brick wall and slide down until I am seated on the dirt floor. I put too much pressure on my ankle and wince at the pain. It flashes through me like a burst of lightning on a hot summer day. I can hear the rumbling thunder in my chest as a scream erupts from my lips.

I was trapped in this space not that long ago. In a strangely similar situation, Will and I fought to survive the brutal attacks my former coven bestowed upon us. It was one of the last moments I had with Will before he died. After we escaped this prison, he left, seeking answers to my predicament. I had so many questions for him about his life, about hybrids, but I always assumed we had more time. Even today, as I rushed to aid the fallen, I didn't consider that tonight would be my last.

The fire grows stronger, more violent, and I am pinned

in place. I cannot move forward, for the fire is inching ever closer. It's lashing at me, teasing my flesh, singeing my clothes. I cannot move backward, for the stone surrounding me has formed a prison. I push against it, but it does not give way.

I suck in deep breath after deep breath but still don't inhale even a small gulp of air. The smoke forms a thick film on my tongue, and I squirm at the bitter taste it leaves in my mouth. My skin is covered in ash—remnants of the house that protected me all these years. I swipe at the sweat that curdles across my forehead as it mixes with soot.

Just when I think I can't handle the warmth any longer, something in the air just…shifts. It startles my senses all at once, and deep in my gut, the predator stirs. It's a warning. I feel the certainty like a cold splash of water against my torrid skin. It jolts me upright. I sit straighter, peering through the smog. I see no better than I did before, but the feeling is no less gripping.

Something has changed.

The fire has sparked to life, and an entity is claiming this space as its own. The basement may appear empty, but I know I am not alone. I am sure of it.

The fever in the air intensifies tenfold, and I feel it sizzle in my chest, scarring my lungs. I know this is it. This is the moment I must fight back. If I don't, I won't survive this fire.

I throw out my hands, summoning my magic. I call for anything—a burst of air, a stream of water, a grumble from the earth. Anything that might aid me now is all I ask for. But nothing happens. The air shifts slightly as I beckon its wrath. The dirt under my butt simply rumbles in protest. The water sprouting from my palms is merely a trickle, unable to extinguish even embers.

I try again and again—all the while, it is becoming harder to keep my eyes open, to focus on my task at hand. I notice I am slouching now, but I don't remember lolling over. My head is pounding, my lungs burning, and my eyes are brutally dry. I close them, welcoming the dark.

But again, something awakens. The silent presence surrounding me strengthens as I grow weaker, and I know I am seconds away from death.

It feeds off my weakness, growing more powerful with each dying breath I take, but I refuse to fall victim to this invisible killer.

In a last, desperate attempt to seem formidable, I intend to shout a spell laced with obscenities, knowing this is an absolutely tragic way to die. But still, I suck in a deep gust of air, Latin incantation in mind. But instead of hexing my attacker, I am choking. My lungs spasm, hacking involuntarily and so violently, I fall over.

I claw at the dirt, and the deeper I dig, the cooler it becomes. I continue, seeking shelter or refuge among the earth, accomplishing nothing more than digging my own gravesite. I pile a small mound before me, knowing it is not enough to smother the flames, but I continue until I can't bear it any longer.

Lying on the ground, I open my heavy eyelids to see a figure walking closer. It morphs as it approaches, as if it too is made from smoke and fire rather than flesh and bone. It withstands the heat with strength I envy.

The more I look at it, the more fearful I become. It appears tall and wispy, a dark, shadowy presence that makes the amulet at my clavicle rattle with excitement.

I know I have no other choice, so I grab on to my amulet,

squeezing it tightly. I lower my defenses, summoning the magic encased within, allowing it to escape its prison just this once, and it explodes from my chest, erupting through my mouth as I scream so loud the foundation shakes.

I harness just enough power to clear the path before me. A tornado of swirling dirt billows all around me, smothering the flames, offering a false sense of security. Without looking back, without making eye contact with whatever creature was hidden in the shadows, I run for the stairs, ascending with experienced ease.

From behind, I hear it laugh, the sound malevolent and ghastly. It's so deep and ominous, it makes my heart melt in my chest—I am certain whatever that thing was, it is the embodiment of evil. And I was locked in the basement with it.

Somehow, it knows me. It wants me. And I know escaping the basement is only the beginning.

"Ava?" someone says, catching my attention as I burst through the closet door. I nearly trip over my feet as I spin around.

I turn to see Jasik, and I collapse against him, finding strength in his embrace. We sit for only a moment as I gather my breath, lungs happily filling with oxygen, before he pulls away, ignoring my protests.

"We have to leave," Jasik says, his voice urgent.

"But I still haven't found them yet," I say, pleading with him.

I know she isn't in this house, but it feels wrong to retreat. I'm still convinced I heard her cries, even though I am sure that was a cruel trick inflicted by whatever monstrosity resides in that basement. After all the horrific things my coven did in that basement, I wouldn't be surprised if yet another evil entity existed—and now it's become my problem.

"You don't understand," Jasik says. "This was no accident. Humans are talking. They saw someone—a man. They claim he started the fire."

"A man? But who? Why?" I ask, a million questions looping endlessly in my mind. If this man started the fire, then what was in the basement with me?

"I don't know, but we intend to find out," he says.

I nod, and he leads us through the kitchen and into the dining room. I glance back, watching the house I grew up in burn. My eyes sting with tears, but I wipe them away quickly.

As we exit through the sliding glass doors, I catch sight of myself in the shards of broken mirror scattered across the floor. Covered in soot and clothes singed, I can see that I very nearly died today. But that isn't what concerns me.

While in the basement, I tried to use my magic, but I couldn't. I'm not so sure my inability to summon the elements was because of my lack of strength. I fear something far worse was at play.

I was trapped by a force more powerful than me—a *hybrid*. This was no simple fire. Magically infused, it was lit to lead me here, to discover the disappearance of my coven. Whoever lit it targeted me by threatening the weakest parts of my soul—my inherent, unshakable love for those who granted me life. We may not be on speaking terms, and we might not be considered allies, but my duty to protect Darkhaven runs deep. Its hold is something I can never escape.

But my panic runs even deeper than that, knowing someone new in town—who has made it clear he's targeting me specifically—doesn't hold my attention as long as it should. I am struck by something far worse, far more vicious.

I can *feel* the dread, the horror strewn across my face, but when I look at myself in the mirror, I don't see it. Instead, the vampire looking back at me is smiling, with tiny black veins threading across her skin. My crimson irises are glistening mischievously, as though the girl behind the mirror knows that this is only the beginning.

My reflection laughs at me. I hear the perverse sound echoing all around me as silent whispers meant only for me, and it sounds like a thousand murderous cackling crows.

FOUR

Sitting on the edge of my bed, I stare at my palm. The emblem burned into my flesh from touching the scorched doorknob is gone, having healed over long before I even returned to the manor, but the psychological pain still lingers. It's an everlasting sting born from my inability to protect my childhood home. There are certain things I am accepting in this life as inevitable, but being a failure is not one of them.

I ball my fist, not wanting to look at it any longer. My pristine, mark-free skin mocks my pain, and that only infuriates me further.

As soon as we returned home, I excused myself, craving a hot shower over communication—a rarity for me. I could tell the others were irritated with me and my desire to escape— after all, Jasik was the sole vampire who understood just how bad things had gotten—but I didn't care. I needed space.

Usually, I am all for talking things out. That's how we learn, we grow. That is how we break free from the prejudices instilled at birth. For the past several months, I have wanted nothing more than to have a conversation with the vampires and witches of Darkhaven. A sit-down chat to just let it all out, to clear the air. Admitting our misdeeds was supposed to be the first step to an alliance, but that never came to pass.

Ever since I hexed the witches and lost friends, I have been slowly shutting down, building walls around me and my far-too-breakable heart. I have been keeping secrets and avoiding difficult conversations. This is not like me, and as much as I want to chalk it up to a bad case of survivor's guilt, I'm not so sure that is why I suddenly feel ... *different*.

My mind flashes back to that sinister reflection. Seeing myself grinning back at me, when I know I most certainly was *not* smiling, is just further proof that something awful is about to happen. Spirit is awake and aware, and I have not been heeding her call. Now, there will be hell to pay.

After I shower and change, tossing my singed clothes into the wastebasket, I'm still not ready to talk about what happened in that house. I decide since I have been stalling this whole time, what's another hour? Eventually, I will have to go downstairs—after all, I am famished—and explain how doomed we all are, but right now, this very second, I'm just not ready to admit that. As much as I hate failure, I seem to be spectacularly good at defeat.

The others are waiting for me downstairs, growing more irritable by the second. I step closer to my bedroom door, pressing my ear against the solid wood. They mumble, desperate to keep their voices low enough to outsmart my heightened senses. I may not catch every word, but I do not miss the doubt or concern in their words.

Everyone is there—the other four hunters and Holland—and I imagine they are arguing about how I can't hide forever. I snort at the idea that *this*—me hiding—is our drama for the evening. If only they knew just how bad things can get ...

Even though I know I should put on a brave face and head downstairs, I step away, lingering back, not wanting to face their wrath. It's the questions I fear. Not just theirs. But also *mine*. I have so many, and every second I spend hashing out the details of what happened after I abandoned Jasik and Malik in favor of saving my mother, I am no closer to answers—and it's answers we all need.

I may not be able to figure out what happened after the house was set on fire, but I certainly have no issues coming up with even more questions or outlandish scenarios.

Who is the man the humans believe started the fire? Why did he target my former house? How did I hear voices yet find no one inside? What happened in the basement, when the fire intensified so fiercely and so quickly that magic *must* have been involved? Does that mean that man is aware of the existence of magic? Or was he not even human to begin with? It wouldn't be the first time a witch or vampire was mislabeled as human. What will happen now that I've accessed the power of the dark entity within the amulet? What about the crows and my nightmares? Are they connected to what happened today?

But more importantly, I still don't know where my mother is. I know what my nestmates will ask—they probably have similar questions—but I can't answer them. Instead, I am left to battle myself.

I don't know what happened at that house!

I scream the words internally, even though I know it isn't enough. It will not stop my head from spinning or my heart from exploding.

I might not know what happened there, but I know what I heard.

I heard their cries!

Again, I scream the words, but they fall silent upon my lips, just as the witches' screams fell upon deaf ears—everyone's ears but mine, that is.

It was not my imagination.

Yet I searched every room, every floor, opening every single door in that house. I found no one...

I repeat myself, but this time, I speak aloud—softly but firmly—as if even I need convincing.

"It wasn't my imagination."

Where is my mother?

If she wasn't at home, where was she? Why would she be anywhere else at that time of night? Considering the hex placed upon her, she wouldn't have risked being out at night. She is smarter than that. She would have stayed home as soon as the sun set.

It doesn't make sense!

I plop onto my bed, resting my elbows against my thighs as I bury my face in my palms. I scratch at my scalp, but no matter how hard I try to dig for answers, my mind is still blank. Nothing makes sense—not my dreams, not the crows, not the cackling I hear in the depths of my soul. I am terrified to look myself in the mirror because I fear *she* will look back at me. That girl I saw in the shards of broken glass bore my face, but she was not me.

I hate to admit it, but life was a lot easier when I wasn't speaking to my mother. I didn't worry about her safety because I trusted she had the knowledge and good judgment to take care of herself.

I like to think she is with friends—maybe another coven member—and she probably hasn't thought about me since we formally cut ties. Even as our home burned, rubble turning to ash, she likely never thought about the fact that this was my childhood home, and in the time it took to strike a match, everything from my former existence was just . . . gone.

I sigh, squeezing my eyes shut so tightly I am convinced the motion can erase the last several hours of my life. It doesn't work. I try again and again. I stop only when I hear the door.

Jasik smiles weakly and walks over to me. I don't know how long I have been here, avoiding them, but I notice how much quieter it is downstairs. The echoing voices that plagued me earlier aren't wafting through the halls, and suddenly I feel an unbearable amount of loneliness, as if everyone on the planet simply vanished.

My sire sits on the bed beside me and grabs my hand, tethering his long fingers with mine. We are linked in so many invisible ways; sometimes, it's nice to feel our physical connection too.

My body tingles where our skin meets, and I feel my cheeks heat. Our bond might not grant Jasik true control over my actions, but he absolutely affects my emotions—in all the best belly-warming and heart-fluttering ways. I have come to relish these sensations. They make me feel normal. Like he's just a boy. And I'm just a girl. We are happy and in love, and we have the rest of our lives to explore what that truly means.

But then I blink, and I am cast out of our fairy tale wonderland and thrust into a world cloaked in shadows.

"You can come downstairs now," Jasik says.

He smiles halfheartedly. I know his words were meant as a soft joke, an easy way to better my mood, but they sting nonetheless. Apparently my cowardice is noticeable to *everyone*.

All the warm, fuzzy feelings nestled in my gut stop swirling at his words, and I shake my head.

"I'm not ready yet," I say painfully.

"I told them not to push you," he says. "I explained how hard this is for you."

I smile when I look at him, but I don't know what to say. True, seeing my childhood home on fire—and nearly dying there myself—has taken a toll on me, but I imagine I don't have many more chances. I have risked a lot over these past several months, and the cost is more than most can bear.

"I'm sorry, Ava," Jasik whispers. "I can't imagine how difficult that must have been for you."

I swallow hard, my mouth suddenly dry. All at once, I feel the heat of the flames against my skin. I feel raw, exposed. I smell my flesh burning as the fire licks my skin. I dab at my forehead with my free hand and notice how hot the room has become since Jasik entered.

"I promise we'll find answers," he continues when I don't respond.

"I know," I choke out, hating that my voice sounds so weak and squeaky.

My heart is pounding in my chest, making me light-headed and woozy. My stomach tightens, squeezing my innards and twisting until they nearly become goo. Why am I having such a visceral reaction to this? Jasik is far from confrontational, but my skin is buzzing at his contact—and no longer in a good way.

"Holland wanted me to tell you that he plans to do some research," Jasik says.

"On the fire?" I ask. I lick my lips, finding them dry, chapped. At this point, I welcome his help.

Jasik shakes his head.

His thumb swirls invisible patterns against my skin, and I focus on that small movement, letting the world around me disappear. Maybe if I have something to ground me, this will all feel easier.

"On your dreams, the crows," Jasik says, interrupting my thoughts.

I suck in a sharp breath and hold it, waiting for his next question. I don't need to be psychic to know where this is going.

But I'm not ready—I'm not ready for this conversation. I avoided the others for this very reason. Not only do I not have the answers the vampires seek, but I am also losing my grasp on reality. How else can I explain my sinister reflection?

"Do you want to tell me about that?" Jasik asks. "About your nightmares?"

His voice is delicate, barely a whisper. I know he is coaxing me into submission, into honesty, and even though he deserves to know, *needs* to know, speaking the words aloud hurts. Every time I think about those dreams, I feel the reality of them like a blade to the heart. Denying their truth was a novice mistake— one I am too experienced to have made—but it was all I could handle. But will he understand that? Will the others?

"I watch you die," I whisper. "Every night. A million different ways. It always ends the same."

Jasik is silent as he considers my confession. When he finally exhales, the sound is gentle, slow, and it eases the tension in my body. It almost sounds like acceptance, like *forgiveness*. Until this moment, I didn't realize how desperately I needed that.

I knew it would come to this—my admission. As soon as I go downstairs, the floodgates will open, and I will be forced to admit yet more mistakes and deal with the consequences of my choices. The vampires have granted me more trust than I deserve, but eventually, they will have had enough. I fear this is that moment.

It was far too easy to convince myself my visions were

the result of an overactive imagination. I meant no harm, but that doesn't lessen my blunder. I knew better. I may be a newborn vampire, but I have been a spirit witch my entire life. I know the signs. A vision here or there can be easily missed, but nightly dreams with the same outcome... I was foolish. Steadfast in my pursuit of happiness, I was willing to risk everything for child's play.

"I make the same mistakes every time," I admit. "I keep too much from you."

"You do, but I understand this is difficult for you. You have been alone for a long time, Ava. Did your coven ever trust you or your visions?"

I shake my head, words just out of reach. The truth is, they never believed in me. I was always a novice, even if I didn't make as many stupid mistakes as I do now. They never thought I was worthy enough.

"You are this distrusting because of the way you were raised. I can't fault you for your behavior. It will take time for you to realize that we only want to see you succeed as a vampire, to enjoy the second chance you were given."

"The others won't understand," I say.

"They aren't..." Jasik sighs heavily. "Well, they aren't happy about it, but they know transitioning is difficult. This isn't a quick process. Becoming a vampire isn't merely physical. Your entire being is changing. Your psychological makeup and even your emotions are affected by this. I promise they will forgive you."

"Are you upset with me?" I ask. I hate that the others are angry, but right now, I care more about Jasik's opinion of me.

"I won't deny that your lack of trust hurts. I want you to confide in me. I want to share your burdens, to carry them for you in every way I can. But I won't force you to bare yourself to me. I will wait until you're ready," Jasik says.

"I'm sorry," I whisper. "I promised I wouldn't keep secrets anymore, and I hid this from you."

"Let's not consider this a secret, then," Jasik says plainly.

I furrow my brow. "What do you mean?"

"I think the reason you didn't tell me about your visions isn't because you wanted to keep them from me. I think you couldn't accept the outcome. Sometimes it's easier to pretend things aren't real. I'm not exactly a newborn vampire, Ava. I've seen and done a lot of things I don't want to talk about, so I'm not surprised these visions were too difficult to mention."

I don't miss the fact that he referred to my nightmares as *visions*—not once but *twice*. He's right: labeling them as what they are is a reality I'm not yet ready to face.

I *know* my dreams were visions. I can admit that to myself now, but I couldn't then. Not after everything that happened. Not after everyone we lost. But hearing that aloud, *talking* about them and discussing action, is just too much right now. Between fearing for Jasik's life, worrying about my mother, deciphering the crows, fearing the evil entity I must protect, and wondering who the mysterious man is, I am running out of sanity. There is only so much of me to go around.

Feeling suffocated by the truth of his words, I stand abruptly, pulling my arm free from his grasp. He releases me easily, not daring to force a conversation I'm not ready for or pin me in place until I can talk about it. He understands even broken wings yearn to soar.

I take several steps away, my mind swirling, the fire in my belly matching the intensity from earlier today. My chest burns, and the heat there is all I can think about.

Too much is happening too suddenly. I feel as though I am being pulled in every direction and my skin is ripping away. My body feels heavy, my limbs numb.

"I'll be okay, Ava," Jasik says. His voice is soothing, but it is no match for my raging emotions.

I close my eyes, and a memory consumes me. I see him—Jasik, my lover, my sire—bursting into flames, and before I can react, the wind carries away his ashes. Although he is forever out of reach, I stumble forward, frantic in my attempt to reach him, to grab hold of what remains.

I never catch him.

I never save him.

In these dreams, I am never the hero.

I open my eyes, a newfound rage springing to life. I am shaking, skin hot from anticipation of what's to come. I feel it rising within me, a familiar sensation I haven't experienced in weeks.

"We don't know that," I say, snapping. I don't know what's worse—denying we have a problem or pretending our problem is easily handled. Again, my visions aren't being taken seriously. Jasik is waving away my concern just as the witches used to.

My voice is angry and harsh, and I watch Jasik wince. Maybe my truth, my doubt, is finally too much for *him* to handle.

Something inside me speaks. It reminds me that in the end, I am always alone. Its voice is deep and dark, and after it tells me that eventually even my sire will abandon me, it laughs. I turn away from Jasik, keeping my gaze on the ground, not wanting him to see how much that truth upsets me.

"Your dreams are warnings, are they not? Now that I

know, I'll be careful. We can beat this—together."

"It's not that easy, Jasik," I hiss. "My visions aren't always preventable."

The chain at my neck rattles, the amulet warming against my skin. Jasik doesn't seem to notice it, so I believe it's in my mind—yet another way my imagination is playing tricks on me. I can still hear that laugh—the low, bellowing cackle that makes my insides squirm. It's all around me now, growing stronger by the second.

I pretend we aren't in my room. We aren't talking about Jasik's impending death because I never envisioned it. Maybe I never even had any nightmares at all. Maybe I made those up too. Maybe I was just seeking attention, like my mother used to say.

"All we can do is try," he says.

The jingling sound from my necklace is echoing all around me, vibrating off the walls and bouncing around my mind. I feel it bubble in my gut, swarming in circles until it spills from my mouth.

"Just trying is not good enough!" I shout.

I open my eyes, not wanting to be alone in the dark. I'm angry, and as I lift my gaze to meet my reflection, I see her glaring back at me. I gasp, jaw ajar, but she smiles at me, eyes gleaming, mouth upturned like a curling snake.

She reaches her arm up and angles her head to the side so she is just off-center. Jasik appears behind me as he approaches, slowly, cautiously, but I revert my attention back to my reflection.

She lifts her hand, index finger erect and the others curled back, and discreetly, slowly, she draws the nail across my neck in a straight, unfailing line. When she glances at

Jasik, I release my rage.

Stomping toward the mirror, I smash my fist against the glass, watching as it breaks into a thousand tiny, spider-webbed pieces. Fragments of glass fall to the tabletop, and I swipe my arms forward, flinging the particles until they scatter across the room.

When I look at my reflection, she is no longer smiling. That girl is gone. Instead, I stare at myself, and I look as scared and as broken on the outside as I feel on the inside.

Jasik is directly behind me now. His presence always sends a rush of sensations coursing through my body—from the way the air shifts to the way his cool embrace envelopes me. I am irate, and my fear for his safety overwhelms me.

I don't want him to see me this way—so erratic and hostile—but I can't help it. I have lost so much—my family, my friends. I have only recently gotten back my magic, my vampirism. How much more can I handle without breaking down for good?

From behind, Jasik wraps his arms around me, planting his palms squarely against my stomach. His fists bunch the fabric of my T-shirt, exposing the soft, pale skin of my lower abdomen. In the mirror, I watch where his hands touch me, grazing my skin, turning my fury into desire.

I spin around to face him, nestling my body against his. He is tall and fit, a solid frame against my much softer body. It appears we are opposite in every way. He is the calm to my storm, the reason to my rash.

"I can't lose you too," I whisper, burying my face against him.

"I'll never leave you," he whispers, his breath bristling the hair at my scalp.

He lowers at the exact moment I stand on my tiptoes, our lips brushing. And all at once, the pain, the fear, the anxiety falls away, birthing a longing, a desire rooted so deeply, I feel it from the pads of my toes to the depths of my soul.

I am dreaming. I know this because I'm watching myself sleep. Standing beside my bed, I stare at my body. It is curved against Jasik, nestled under the thin covers. The ceiling fan overhead causes my hair to flutter in the breeze, but it does not wake me.

I reach forward to touch my sire, stopping short of making actual contact. Something distracts me. The growl is low, but I am certain I heard it. And it came from this room.

I spin around, but my bedroom begins to fall away, disappearing like shadows in the night. From where I stand beside the bed, I see it. It hides in the corner, eyes bright and glowing, golden in color and heart-stopping in ferocity.

It steps out, taking a slow, confident stride toward me. The beast looks similar to a wolf but is much larger than any I have ever seen. The closer it comes, the farther back I walk, until I am flush against the wall. Trapped. Still, I try to mold into the drywall, melt away, become one with the house, but it's no use.

I feel its snout against my skin, but I don't see it. I have long since closed my eyes, pretending that such action can actually save me from this monster. It is cold and wet, and each abrupt, sharp exhale makes me jolt upright until I am standing on my tiptoes, praying for an escape.

I hear the glass from my window shatter and feel the air in the room shift. I open my eyes to find the beast gone. In its place is the gargoyle, the very one I greet day after day. No longer small or stone, it is towering, with a wingspan larger than me. It releases a loud, shrieking bellow, and the wolf howls at the moon.

When the wolf ceases its struggle, succumbing to the superior wrath of the gargoyle, they both glance at me.

Watching. Waiting. As though even they are unsure of how I will react.

I make eye contact with the gargoyle, and its shimmery silver irises slowly fade to black.

I am alone now. No longer in my bedroom, I escaped, finding refuge in another time, another place. My dreams always happen this way—sudden and short-lived, rash and unsteady. One moment, I am here. The next, I'm not.

I try to assess where I am, but the longer I remain in this place, where spirit resides, the more confused I become. The longer I wait, the harder it is to return to my body. Even though I know this, I *know* I should return to the manor and wake myself from this dream, I don't move. Because I haven't been shown the reason for this vision. Spirit is waiting until the right moment to offer me a glimpse into the future, and I need to know why. *Why* is it taking so long?

I am breathing heavily now, willingly allowing my uncertainties to consume my emotions. I know I shouldn't. I need to be smart, to watch carefully for the signs from spirit. But my anxiety has me by the throat, and it has no intention of releasing me.

The darkness surrounding me is closing in, as though it is alive. It shudders and echoes, springing to life, and somehow, I know it enjoys my fear. It feeds off it, trapping me in this silent abyss. The evil that lurks here wants me to join it. I stand my ground, unwavering as an agent of good.

I listen to the rapid bursts of my own breathing, but I see nothing. No sign from spirit. No warning cleverly coated in some obscure vision. The night feels endless, an eternal pit of despair. And it has waited for me for such a long time.

"We're trapped," someone whispers, and I jerk at the sound, truly believing I was alone. I gasp at the intrusion.

She keeps her voice low, a nearly silent hiss. A plea. I can't see her, but I know the sound of her voice.

"Hikari?" I say. I hear her shuffle toward me, but I still cannot see her. I wonder if she is even there. Maybe my mind is playing tricks on me. The darkness can influence the weak in many ways, and unfortunately, I *am* weak.

"Ava, what do we do?" she continues. Her panic has increased tenfold. I understand she is looking to me for guidance, but for what? What has happened? I feel as though the veil is only partially lifted. It was enough for Hikari to sneak through, but nothing else. How can I guide her if I do not know where we are? I'm not even sure she's really here.

"Hikari, is that you?" I repeat, still unsure if this is simply a game, a trick. Is this a vision or my imagination? An incorrect assumption could cost Hikari her life. I need to know if this is why spirit brought me here.

She speaks again, but I don't understand her words. I am slipping away, but I'm not ready to go. She sounds fear-stricken, muffled and murky. I use the steady beats of her heart as an anchor, hoping they will ground me in place, and suddenly, I sense her. She is near. So close I believe I can reach out and touch her. I try this, stumbling forward and tripping over the air that has quickly become solid.

Hikari is beside me now, steadying my fall. I grab on to her. Knowing she is here with me calms my anxiety. I feel stronger,

I think smarter. I become the warrior who always lived inside.

She looks different, tired and weak. She appears wounded, but I don't smell blood. She is exasperated as she carries me through a labyrinth of tunnels—all ending so abruptly it's as if they weren't there to begin with.

Where are we?

"We have to keep moving," she pleads, keeping her voice low. "We need to find a way out."

"But we're trapped. I thought we were trapped," I say, reminding her of our situation.

She needs to tell me more, to explain what has happened. Where are we? Why is she hurt? Why is she still holding on to me? Her grasp is so tight around my waist, she alone is what's keeping me upright.

Hikari looks at me, so close I can finally see her clearly. Her eyes are bulging, tears streaming down her face. Her face is smeared with blood, and her hair is in disarray. She gasps, tries to speak, but sound never leaves her lips.

And then she's gone. Like the darkness, she dissipates, blending into the blackness that surrounds me.

I blink and I'm outside, free of the caves that confined me only moments ago. The sky is light and bright, and I shield my vision as I gaze up. The brightness burns my retinas, and tears fall freely. Daringly, I peer through squinted lids. The sun is overhead, but the earth is cast in shadows.

Confused, I look back, still hoping to find Hikari beside me, but she is gone. I remember her disappearing. Being there one moment, gone the next. I watched her leave as the vision changed, but still, I shout her name and spin in circles, surprised to be alone.

I stop moving and focus on my surroundings. I am in

Darkhaven, standing in the middle of a familiar street. The storefronts are dark, the showrooms empty. The woods are at my left, the town on my right. And even though I see no one, I feel a presence.

Lurking. Watching.

It's always there, waiting until I close my eyes to make itself known. No matter the place, no matter the situation, it's there.

I call to Hikari, praying it's her, but she never responds. I shout again, telling the onlooker to make himself known. I feign confidence and strength, even as I shake and quiver. Something about this place feels chilling and unruly, like death resides here. And death knows I'm here too.

From behind me, I hear my name. The girl who speaks to me is someone I have never met. Even before I turn to look at her, I know this to be true.

I spin and see her, and she is talking to me, but her features are blurred. A faceless figure unknown to me, she is nothing but a small, thin frame with unwavering strength. It practically seeps from her being and fills the air around her.

She speaks again, but instead of focusing on her words, I listen to her voice. Surely I must know her. Why else is she in my dreams?

"Hikari?" I whisper, even though I know this person is not my friend.

Instead of answering my call, the girl screams and points to something behind me, and I feel it. Whatever it is, whatever terrifies her, is there—so close I can hear its raspy breathing. It is heavy and hoarse, and it says my name.

A knot forms in my throat, and I know this is what spirit wanted me to see, and even though every cell of my body is screaming at me to run, I don't. I fight the desire to flee by twisting, contorting my frame until I am face-to-face with . . . nothing.

It's gone.

But in the distance, I see something else. Someone catches my eye. A rogue vampire smiles back at me—his teeth pointy and bright, stained pink by innocent blood. His skin is so pale it's luminescent. His deep-blue veins form spider webs across his body, and as I look at him, he raises his arm, extending his index finger.

He swipes his nail across his neck, piercing his skin. Deep trails of crimson slide down until they pool around the collar of his shirt, staining it bloodred. And he is laughing—a hypnotic, ghostly snicker that makes my own blood run cold.

I step forward, mesmerized by the sight before me. No longer claimed by the desire to run, I hold out my hand to the rogue, who cackles as the tears drip down my cheeks, splashing on the cement at my feet.

And I call to him, my voice so low, so whispery soft, I'm not sure he can hear me from where he stands.

"Jasik."

FIVE

With a steaming mug of blood in hand, Holland greets me as soon as I walk into the kitchen. He smiles widely, his gaze flicking between his breakfast offering and me. Unable to silence my rumbling stomach, I comply, sliding into the seat in front of him.

"Morning," I say as I grab the mug.

Holland responds, but I don't hear him. Focused solely on my breakfast, I drink the warm, thick liquid quickly.

When I'm done, I lick my lips and set down the mug. With breakfast done, I'm already itching to leave, but I have a feeling escaping the manor won't be easy. Holland is eying me curiously, and I know any hope I had of leaving without answering his pressing questions is moot.

"You had a vision again, didn't you?" he asks.

Apparently we're diving right in. Pleasantries be damned.

I shrug in response, my mind swirling, still attempting to decipher just what spirit was trying to tell me. True, I had a dream, but it's never that simple. Just because I had the vision doesn't mean I'm ready and able to discuss it.

"Ava, I might not be a spirit user, but I am knowledgeable," he says. "Let me help you."

"I'm not sure you can," I admit.

Holland sighs heavily. "Stop being a spirit hog and share

some details. You never know. I may hold all the answers." He taps his temple playfully, a grin creasing his smooth cheeks.

I sigh sharply, caving.

"It started in my room," I say. "I woke up, and I was by my bed, watching us sleep. Something else was in the room with me. A wolf or something."

Holland frowns. "Interesting. Wolves hold a lot of symbolism in our culture. They're one of the most respected and feared animals."

I shake my head. "It wasn't a regular wolf. For one thing, it was a lot bigger. Massive in size. Its fur was so dark it almost completely blended into the shadows. Maybe it did. Its eyes were glowing and golden in color. It had the form of a wolf, but I'm not so sure it was a regular wolf."

Holland recoils, a grimace painted across his face. "Seriously creepy. Are your visions always like this? So dark and detailed?"

"Usually dark but rarely detailed," I say. "Spirit wants to warn me of impending doom, but it's my responsibility to connect the dots."

Holland nods. "I suppose that makes sense. What happens next?"

"The gargoyle out front comes alive and slays the beast," I say, snorting.

Saying it aloud makes it sound far more comical than it was in the moment. I'll admit, I was terrified. It might have seemed like a child's nightmare, but there is something exceptionally horrifying about bearing witness to storybook creatures springing to life—especially when I am unable to protect myself from them.

Holland fights back a snicker, just like I expected him

to. This is the worst part about being a spirit witch. No one understands. Explaining my visions to someone incapable of experiencing that level of pure terror is impossible. Spirit might use symbolism, but rarely does spirit sugarcoat lessons needed to be learned. This makes for unnerving dreams and awkward conversations.

I roll my eyes at Holland's obvious smirk and continue.

"That part makes sense to me. Legend says gargoyles are the vampires' daylight protectors. They turn to stone at night when vampires are awake and able to protect themselves, and they come to life during the day while vampires slumber. I think it was just my imagination getting the best of me."

"I suppose, but why would your subconscious include that in your vision?" Holland asks. "Why now? Why during this particular dream?"

I swallow hard, mentally preparing to admit all my faults. "Because I've been bitter about what happened. When Will and Amicia... When we lost them, it was during daylight hours. If the legend were true, we would have been protected. They wouldn't have died. Maybe we would have had more time. Maybe I could have..."

I sigh and run a hand through my hair before resting my arms atop the table. I clasp my hands together, forming a single fist so solid, so strong, I believe one hard smack against the wood surface will cause it to splinter. And I know I have that sort of rage stored within me, bubbling just beneath the calm, collected exterior I show the world. It's a lie. It's *always* a lie.

I stare past Holland, peering into the backyard. I can see them from here. They're always close, always alone. Cold and hard, a sturdy vision of eternal resilience, their tombstones mock my pain. When I close my eyes and listen deeply, I hear their cries. They sound the same as they did the day they died. That's why I hate the darkness, the shadow. I'm surrounded by it constantly, and when it consumes me, I experience nothing but agony and regret.

Holland grabs hold of my hands, sorrow in his eyes. It's painful to simply look at him. I know the torture I see there is reflected in me. We all carry our heavy loss together, but some bear the weight more than others.

"Ava, legends are complicated. They require a lot of moving parts to work cohesively. Nothing is ever simple when it comes to magic."

I jerk my hands free, needing space. I clear my throat, intending to change the subject. The last thing I need right now is to discuss Will or Amicia or the fact that I still hold a grudge against a stone artifact on our front porch. I don't want to talk about legends, so I settle on my vision.

Sniffling, with arms crossed over my chest as my last protective barrier, I say, "After that, my dream abruptly changed and I was somewhere dark. A tunnel or maybe a cave. I'm not sure. It wasn't familiar to me. I thought I was alone, but then Hikari spoke, and I realized we were stuck there together. We were both injured and scared. She mentioned that we were surrounded, but I didn't sense anyone else. Before I could see more, it changed again. Hikari was gone."

Holland frowns, searching his mind. His eyes are hazy, and he remains unblinking for so long it makes my own eyes water.

"Holland?" I say softly, and he blinks several times as his vision adjusts, focusing on me.

"Sorry. What happened next?"

"I was outside, in downtown Darkhaven. The sun was

out, but it was still dark out. Someone was there, but I couldn't see her face. But she knew me. I could *tell* she knew me, but I didn't recognize her. Her face was blurred."

Holland's brow furrows, and he looks slightly dazed as he contemplates what I've said. This time, I wait for him to speak. Dissecting a spirit witch's dreams isn't like science class.

"I think we can assume the girl in your vision is someone you haven't met *yet* but will meet whenever this vision comes true. That would explain why your astral self didn't recognize her. You haven't seen her yet."

I nod. "Yeah, I guess. That makes sense."

"Did she seem friendly?" he asks. "Was she an ally or a foe?"

I think about the vision, but very little of it focused on her. This is typical of spirit. It never lingers too long on any one aspect. That would make decoding the clues far too easy.

"Honestly, I'm not sure," I say. "I felt okay around her. When something sinister is near, I can feel it in my dream. I know when evil is there, when spirit is warning me about something wicked. I didn't feel that way around her, but that's not to say she's a potential ally. If we do end up meeting, we should be careful around her. The fact that she was in my dream is peculiar enough."

"I agree. We need to be smart about this considering how many dreams you've had of Jasik."

My heart sinks at the mention of my sire's name. The reality that I might lose him is still sinking in.

"Is that all that happened?" he asks.

I glance away, stalling by fidgeting with the empty mug in front of me. How much should I confess? Is it fair to share the final details with Holland before I've even warned Jasik? After all, this is Jasik's life we're talking about. He should be warned first.

But I know the last part of my dream was the part spirit wanted me to see. All of my previous visions involved Jasik dying an immortal's death, but this time, he was reborn as a rogue vampire. That must mean something, but I refuse to believe he would turn rogue.

After I transitioned, Jasik explained to me that becoming a rogue vampire is a choice. Submitting to the innate evil tendencies vampires inherit, rogues succumb to their dark side, choosing to take innocent lives. It's that loss of innocence in the vampire that completes the transformation, and as far as I know, no one has ever reverted back, shedding the rogue nature and being reborn as a vampire, which is why I *know* Jasik would never willingly turn rogue. He values his life too much. He has a nest to protect, a brother, me... He wouldn't just walk away from the life he's built, even if his sire is dead and he's still dealing with that reality, that pain.

"Did you see him die again?" Holland whispers, interrupting my thoughts.

I nod, not meeting his gaze. Internally, I justify I didn't *technically* lie, but I know my eyes will give away my secrets. So I keep my lids hooded by staring at the table. I scratch at the wood with my nail, carving a small crater.

"Ava, I promise, I am working as hard as I can to translate your dreams so we can be better prepared for the moment when it... when it happens."

I suck in a sharp breath. This is the first time I've actually spoken about the dreams as visions, as a reality I will soon face. Hearing the truth in Holland's words forces all the air from my lungs, and I gasp, my chest spasming painfully. I clutch my shirt, bunching the fabric in my palms.

The amulet dangling at my collar burns against my flesh, and I wince at the sudden pain that shoots through me.

"Ava," Holland whispers, but I'm already standing. I rise so quickly my chair falls backward, smacking against the tile floor.

"I can't listen to this," I hiss.

My skin sizzles where the amulet grazes against it, and I gnaw on my lower lip. I haven't told anyone that I summoned the magic in order to escape the fire, and I don't want that revelation to come because the scent of my burning flesh is wafting through the air.

So I run. I tear through the kitchen and into the dining room, dashing down the hall until I reach the front door. I glance back before I close it behind me.

The manor is still silent this early in the night. It's almost peaceful, as if my world isn't crumbling around me as I stand, gasping for air, brushing away the tears.

The others will wake soon, but I've decided that I'll be long gone.

Closing the door, I rest against its solid wood frame, leaning my head against the stained-glass windows at its center. I listen intently, but I never hear Holland approach. I don't expect him to. He knows I need space, time to consider what my visions mean.

I turn, stepping away from the doors, and look into the distance, watching as a mist forms around the forest. The fog will soon be so dense I won't be able to see more than a few feet in front of me, and even though I know it's reckless, I have made my decision. It's the only way I can successfully avoid the others while I wrap my mind around everything that's happened.

I intend to patrol the woods—something I haven't done in more days than I can count. I stopped patrolling after we lost half our nest—some to death, others to the promise of new leadership elsewhere. I was angry with the witches for taking Amicia and Will from me, but a part of me, however small, thought there wasn't a good reason to continue our patrols. We hunted to protect the town, and that's exactly where the witches resided. If they didn't want a truce, they wouldn't continue to benefit from our patrols. In my mind, it was that simple. Now, I see how misguided I was, how easily I allowed my emotions to manipulate my morals.

I walk to the edge of the porch, the tips of my boots hanging over the step, and I stop. I close my eyes, taking deep breaths and letting the refreshing air wash over me. I feel stronger when I am outside, running through the woods like an uncaged animal. I feel free.

I look to the moon for comfort, and she obliges, allowing her bright, iridescent rays to shine down on me. If I plan to hunt, I must lean on her for strength. I am rusty and distracted, weak and emotional. But I yearn to make her proud, to make them *all* proud.

The vampires aren't happy with me—rightfully so—but if they see I am trying to satisfy the needs of this nest, maybe they will overlook my secrets. I plan to right the wrongs I have made, even if I have to hunt and kill every remaining rogue vampire lurking in these woods to prove my dedication to this nest.

Regardless of how long I stalk this forest, I know Holland will be waiting for me. He understands that I need time. Watching your lover die over and over again—and being the sole witness to the act—takes a toll. I have to carry the weight of that truth, and it's not an easy vision to withstand.

I crouch at the top of the stairs, resting my elbows on my thighs. Our daylight protector—the gargoyle—is perched beside me. Dark gray and stained by years of elemental harassment, he appears fierce and formidable, as though the simple act of snapping my fingertips will bring him forth, awakening him from his slumber to avenge our fallen.

I decide that wouldn't be the case, regardless of Holland's explanation of legends. The gargoyle is made of stone, with sharp angles and striking curves, much like the Victorian manor he presides over. But in my dream, I witnessed his wrath. He sprang to life, protecting me against a beast I never knew I needed to fear.

Unsure of what to believe, I sigh and pat his head, wondering how far my imagination will run wild with the idea that gargoyles truly are alive. I might dream about him again, night after night, and he will become an unwitting participant in this desperate charade to save Jasik's soul.

Cool and smooth, he stares past me, unblinking, unmoving. Never looking but always watching.

"Keep them safe until I return," I whisper, choosing to believe he will obey.

Spring is settling over Darkhaven. The cool breeze has shifted, becoming warmer, more delicate. The harsh reality of the abrupt seasonal change is welcoming, even though it irritates my heightened senses. I scrunch my nose at all the new scents lingering in the air.

The earliest perennial flowers have begun to bloom,

surprisingly withstanding last night's sudden frost. Pops of color burst through the forest as if someone intentionally planted a path of tulips to lead me through the darkness.

They glisten in the night, sparkling against the moonlight. Some are bright red; others are yellow and orange and purple. I linger, admiring the multicolored ones. I bend down to pick one and inhale its sweet aroma. Flowers remind me of herbs, and herbs remind me of home—the very one I lost. My heart burns at the thought.

As I walk, I carry the flower with me, plucking each petal and offering it to the earth as I hike deeper into the woods.

There is a crunch under my feet familiar from previous months I patrolled these woods, but it is pliable now. As winter begins to hibernate, the world softens and the animals wake. I hear them now, skittering among the brush, returning to their nests and dens. Even in darkness, life emerges victorious. I must remind myself of this. The world might be brutal, but hope can prevail.

With the flower fully plucked, I toss the stem to the ground and focus better on my surroundings. I need to be alert, but all I can think about is my nightmare and how the new man in town might be linked to my visions of Jasik dying.

Spirit was warning me of what's to come, but what part was simply a dream? Which part was simply my imagination? Who was the mysterious girl, and is she linked to the person who burned down my house?

I kick at the ground, scuffing my boots. Broken twigs soar through the air, landing in a heap several feet away.

The farther I am from the manor, the less my skin burns each time the amulet sways against the raw flesh there. I still haven't dared to look at it. I can feel it tethering together as it heals itself, and soon, when I do look down, it will appear untouched, unwounded. Only I will know that it's a lie.

I think about that moment in the basement when the smoke intensified so much I couldn't breathe. Somehow, I know I should have died down there. If I hadn't relied on the amulet's strength, I would not be here right now. So even though I know I promised I would never harness the evil entity's power, I can't say I am regretful of my actions.

I glance at the sky, assessing the time from the moon's position. The others should be awake by now. If they haven't already noticed, they will soon realize I'm not there. Holland will tell them about our conversation. He'll explain how I ran out, and they will argue about my emotional state, about my visions. They'll be angry with me for not being there to talk about the situation. What they won't expect is that I have no remorse for leaving so hastily.

A girl can only handle so much, and right now, my basket is overflowing. I'm at the edge, staring into the abyss, and begging the universe not to push me into the darkness.

But even I know that's a fool's dream.

"Hello, pretty lady," someone says, interrupting my thoughts.

I freeze, the tiny hairs covering my body standing on end, alerting me to the speaker's presence. If I weren't so completely overwhelmed by my anxiety—after all, it's not exactly easy to sneak up on a hybrid—I might consider internally chastising my *supposedly* heightened senses for their delayed reaction.

Of course, I don't do this. Instead, I feign confidence in the way only I can. I spin on my heels, face masked with the best death-dagger glare I can offer.

One thing I have learned from all my training sessions

with Malik is that presentation in battle is an excellent weapon against opponents. It doesn't matter how emotional I am on the inside. If I look the part of a warrior on the outside, I will instill fear in my enemy with little effort on my part. It's all about playing on the impressions already instilled in their minds, like how wearing a suit automatically makes someone appear successful. I prepare myself to seem fierce and formidable, even if my heart is racing and my mind is hazy.

But as soon as I face him, I lose all confidence. Because the man looking back at me is no stranger at all. I have seen him before. In the depths of my nightmares, he has haunted me for weeks, for months even. He was there before I ever lost Will, before I ever hexed the witches.

This rogue vampire is no stranger at all—and he came for me.

Wearing only pants, the skin of his torso is smooth and pale. His hands are dirty, his jeans scuffed and shredded. His feet are bare, and his toes burrow into the earth as he watches me. I imagine he can see it in my eyes—the recognition, the fear. He knows I remember him, remember the first time we met.

A knot forms in my throat, and I force it down. It remains lodged in my chest, anchoring me to this moment. The rogue chuckles, his sunken eyes sparkling defiantly.

His head is shaved, his face scarred from cuts he must have sustained during the many years before he became a vampire. His irises are burning red, his nose creased by a sharp angle. It must not have been set properly after a break—again, happening before he became a monster.

His lips are pale and dry, and his teeth are stained pink by years of draining the blood of the innocent. Even now, his lips are smeared red, as if he only recently claimed a life.

He smiles at me, and my gaze lands on his dagger fangs. I suck in a sharp breath, but it doesn't budge the boulder implanted in my lungs.

I am terrified of the rogue before me, yet I am unable to run. Rooted in place, frozen by the image of him before me, I simply stare back, replaying the vision I had of him that first night we met.

He first emerged in a nightmare, and even though he promised he was not a dream, I didn't believe him when he told me he was real. Because it shouldn't have been possible. Rogue vampires haven't the capability to enter the astral plane where spirit is most powerful.

But he was there, and he wounded me. Even now, he holds power over me. I grab my arm, clasping my fingers over the spot where he marked my skin that night. The imprint of his strength is long gone, but I still *feel* it—the bruised flesh, the weakened muscle. All from one quick, effortless touch.

The rogue vampire before me is hideous, with malice practically dripping from his fingertips like streams of blood cascading from a gaping wound. As he walks forward, slowly, methodically, the darkness encircling him swarms, coming to life, buzzing all around like hungry bees. The sound grows louder the longer he stares at me, the closer he approaches.

I take a cautious step backward, desperate to distance us, and he shakes his head, *tsk*ing me playfully. With his index finger, he taunts me as it sways side to side.

His eyes narrow, but his lips curve into a smile. I wonder how long he has waited for this moment. Since my dream? Or has he known about my existence long before he conned his way into my visions?

I continue backpedaling until I back into something solid. I don't need to turn around to know another rogue vampire is standing behind me. He growls as I lean against him, nose ruffling my hair as he inhales and exhales deeply. I wonder if he can smell my fear, like a cornered animal watching as a predator closes in on it.

He wraps his hands around my arms and slowly tightens his grip until I wince at the pressure. I wouldn't be surprised if there were more rogues lurking in this forest, and I even play with the idea that they have been stalking these woods, waiting until I finally returned to my nightly patrols. I bet my sabbatical from hunting irked them, which only brings me pleasure.

Not willing to give them the upper hand, I slam my head backward, making direct contact with the rogue's nose. He shrieks and releases me, giving me more than enough space to withdraw my stake and jab it into his chest. It makes contact with his heart, and he sucks in a sharp breath before bursting into ash.

I return my gaze to the other rogue, and he makes his anger evident. He releases a ferocious roar that is so loud, so angry, the ground shakes. He thrashes forward, and I grip my stake so hard I fear it will snap in two.

The moment he is within striking distance, I leap into the air, twisting above him, flipping effortlessly so that I land behind him. I have practiced this very maneuver on Malik so often I can do it blindfolded.

I plant the sole of my boot into his back, slamming it so hard I hear the distinct sound of bones snapping. I smile as the crack lingers in the air because I know I have him right where I want him.

In my dreams, this rogue might have been my nightmare,

but in real life, *he* will fear *me*.

The rogue stumbles forward, crashing to the ground in a grunting heap. Using the toe of my boot, I push him over. The desire to take his life and to ensure he watches me do so is all-consuming. It bubbles inside me, spilling from my lips in a giddy laugh. The amulet at my chest hums, and I find it calming, strengthening, rejuvenating. It's as if it too is ecstatic over this kill.

But my excitement over gaining the upper hand is quickly extinguished when someone grabs me from behind. Bunching the loose hair from my messy bun in her palm, another rogue vampire appears suddenly, yanking my skull backward so forcefully, I yelp.

Leaning into her attack, I struggle to ease the pain. It relents only when she tosses my limp body to the side like I am nothing more than trash in her way. She growls at me, baring her fangs like a wolf challenging another's territory, but she turns away before finishing the act.

With me out of the way, she jumps to the other rogue's aid, risking her own life to save his. It's clear who the alpha is in this pack, which brings to mind another lesson from Malik. Always kill the alpha first. With the alpha gone, gammas retreat and betas fight for leadership.

"Ava, remember, if you are ever in a tricky situation, find the alpha," he'd said, his words swirling my mind now even though he is dozens of miles away.

I know what I must do, and the thought thrills me. I have never felt so energized while hunting, especially when facing multiple rogues, but I welcome these new feelings, intending to use them to strengthen my magic.

Calling upon the elements, I harness fire. I summon it so

quickly, so easily, the injured rogue glances up as I am already throwing out my arms before me. Flames shoot from my palms, bellowing in waves so intense my skin sizzles at its proximity.

But with my attention focused on the alpha, I am not watching the girl. She screams and leaps forward, putting herself in the path of my fury.

She incinerates in seconds, and my shock is so overwhelming, I lose control of the magic I have summoned. Cut off from the elements, the heatwave is sucked back into my core, and all that remains is a pile of ash and the burnt, crisp brush between the alpha and me.

Still stunned by the vampire's sacrifice, I barely notice the alpha has already jumped to his feet, his snapped spine healing far too quickly for my liking.

He pounces, gliding through the air and landing on top of me. Pinned in place, I struggle to free myself. He is stronger than I expected him to be. With one hand controlling my wrists, he wraps the other around my throat. The thought that he can end my life in one swift jerk thrills me, even though I know it shouldn't. I know I should be afraid, but I'm not.

He leans forward, our noses touching. "I didn't expect you to have a death wish."

His pungent breath cascades over my face, his spit spraying across my skin. Bile rises in my chest, but I force it down.

"Let me go," I seethe.

I think we are both surprised by my strength, because his eyes widen ever so slightly before he smiles and releases a deep, loud laugh.

But before I can react, he stops. Frowning, his gaze flickers to something in the distance. With my pounding heart and the blood rushing to my head, I can't focus well enough to acknowledge what he hears, but from the look of annoyance splashed across his face, I can assume tonight didn't go as planned.

Just as I'm about to call out, assuming whatever stole the rogue's attention could be beneficial to my current situation, the alpha strengthens his hold over my throat. He squeezes so tightly, I am completely cut off from my air supply.

As I struggle to breathe, the hiss escaping my throat sounds nothing like me, yet I know that weak, subtle whine is coming from me. My vision blurs, my eyes swelling with tears.

The amulet heats so intensely, I am afraid my chest will melt and it will fall to the earth below, turning my body into a puddle of goo. Strangely, the rogue doesn't seem to notice the fire growing against my chest, and I pray it stays that way. Even if he takes my life, I cannot relinquish the power of the amulet to him.

"Next time, you won't be so lucky," he seethes.

He releases me. The crushing weight of his body on top of mine is gone. My lungs fill with air, and they convulse painfully as they struggle to bring me back from the brink of unconsciousness.

I turn onto my side, hacking and sucking in sharp bursts of air. Dirt coats my lips as I try to claw my way toward safety, still unconvinced he is really gone.

But suddenly, I am no longer on the ground. I am floating through the air with only the pressure of something solid at my back. I roll against him, and he cradles me, brushing away the dirt and hair that has clung to my skin.

"Jasik," I whisper.

I stare into his eyes, but as he looks back at me, my lover

is gone. All I can see is the rogue vampire he is destined to become.

SIX

Jasik smiles at me, and the vision of him turning rogue disappears. I reach for him, sliding my fingertips across the sharp angle of his jawline. How can something so beautiful actually exist? How can something so precious to me be taken away so effortlessly in my dreams?

"Were you attacked?" he asks, setting me down.

I wobble as I stand, but the fog in my head is slowly clearing. Rather than standing on my own, I allow Jasik to linger. His hand grips my waist firmly, almost possessively.

I nod, not speaking the words aloud, and press my index fingers against my temples. My vision might have cleared, but there is still a throbbing within my skull, and it worsens with every second. I imagine this particular pain won't cease until I find and kill that rogue vampire.

Being bested is exceptionally annoying. It's even worse to be beaten in such an embarrassing way. He had me pinned down, easily subduing me, and if Jasik hadn't come for me... I shake my head, hoping to clear it. Because the last thing I need plaguing my thoughts is a rogue vampire ripping out my throat.

"What is it? Was it rogue vampires or...?" he asks, trailing off.

He glances past me, squinting against the darkness, but I know that final vampire is long gone. The only thing lingering is Jasik's unfinished sentence.

"Or?" I repeat, making it clear in my tone that I want him to finish.

He meets my eyes, but something is different about him. His exterior is defensive and formidable, but there is a softness in his gaze meant solely for me.

"Or witches," he says firmly. "Was it the witches who attacked you?"

I swallow hard. Of course he meant witches. Who else would attack me in the woods? It must be rogues or witches.

I shake my head and admit, "Rogues. One got away."

"At least you're safe," he says. "That's all that matters."

"He will come back," I warn. Noting this is moot. Jasik knows the rogue will return. They *always* come back for me. They are also contenders for the Worst Timing Ever Award.

"They always come back, Ava," Jasik says, mirroring my thoughts. "What's important is that we survive when they return."

"I know," I say, feeling ashamed.

Once again, visions of how easily the rogue subdued me flash in my mind. I break eye contact with my sire and step away from him, desperately needing space between us.

"Tell me about them," Jasik asks.

Something in his tone alerts me to his seriousness. He is stiff, a bit harsh, in the way he orders me to relay details about a fight I have no intention of reliving. Still, I obey.

"There were three, I think," I say. I hate that there could have been more and I was simply too distracted to notice. "I killed the first easily. He stood behind me, and I was able to quickly stake him. I used fire magic to kill the other."

I frown, remembering the moment I summoned magic.

I'm still shocked that she took a bullet meant for the other. While I can understand the unyielding desire to protect your sire, that emotion seems so unlike rogue vampires. My only encounters with them have led me to believe they're merely monsters, and monsters don't make friends.

"What is it? What aren't you telling me?" Jasik asks.

I shake my head. "Nothing. There were just the three."

"I know something about them was different," Jasik says. "Ava, as good as you are at keeping secrets, I am better at noticing that you're hiding them. So I will ask again, what was different?"

I cross my arms over my chest, sinking into my body for comfort. Jasik rarely takes such a fierce tone with me, and while I can understand why he would choose this particular moment to play on his role as sire, it irritates me.

"The one I killed with magic took a fireball meant for the other rogue," I say. "That's weird, right?"

Jasik's brow furrows in shock. "Yes. That's quite strange. Rogue vampires rarely showcase such devotion. I'd argue it's almost impossible for them to feel such emotion."

"Well, this one did," I say. "I assumed the rogue she saved was an alpha rogue or something. Her leader. She died to save him."

My voice is soft, the honesty of my words nearly crippling me. Jasik and I both understand why she did what she did, even if it was unusual behavior from a rogue vampire. I know, without a doubt, Jasik would have died to save Amicia if only given the chance, and I would stop at nothing to save him should his life ever truly be in danger. It's the bond we have—the sire bond.

Suddenly, something occurs to me, and I could kick myself

for not thinking of this earlier. After all, the signs were there.

"What if he sired her?" I ask.

"Rogues rarely turn humans," he says. "That requires a great deal of strength."

"But you changed me," I say, confused.

"That was different," he says. "I am not rogue."

I gasp at his words, sucking in a sharp breath. He frowns, noticing the abrupt change in my demeanor. I consider telling him about my last dream, about the night he changed, the night he became a rogue vampire, but I can't. Not yet. Simply hearing him speak about it causes a visceral reaction in my gut, and I'm about ready to spill my breakfast.

"How was that different?" I ask, still needing answers even though we're walking a dangerous path.

"Rogue vampires are driven by their blood lust," Jasik explains. "It would be especially difficult for a vampire suffering from blood lust to *stop* feeding long enough to swap blood. You have to do this at precisely the right moment for the transition to work. Have you ever wondered why the world isn't crawling with vampires? That isn't simply because we aren't *trying* to make vampires. Nest leaders try often, actually. It's because creating a vampire is difficult."

"But the sire bond would explain why she would offer her life in exchange for his," I say.

Jasik considers this, remaining silent. As the seconds tick by, I know I'm right. If that rogue vampire is strong enough to control his blood lust, then we have another serious problem on our hands. Because we've both already agreed that he will come back for me.

"I think we are dealing with a rogue vampire who is much more powerful than any we have ever faced," I admit.

"Why?" Jasik asks. "Because he sired a vampire? Or did something else happen?"

"This particular vampire was in my dream," I say.

Jasik frowns. "Has this ever happened before?"

I shake my head. "I mean, Will entered my dream too, but that makes sense. He was a spirit user as a witch. He had access to the astral plane, but rogue vampires ... That should be impossible."

"Yet somehow he found a way inside," Jasik says.

"The only thing that makes sense is a witch granted him access, but still, that is a bit farfetched."

"Because witches and vampires can't be friendly?" Jasik asks, grinning. His all-knowing smile causes me to roll my eyes.

"Holland is different. I was different. *You* are different. We aren't rogue vampires, Jasik. No witch would willingly work with rogue vampires. That idea is just *insane*. Rogue vampires are the very creatures we want to eradicate. We are born biased, and we spend our lives fighting them."

"True, we may not be rogue, and we are far more civilized than you considered before you became one of us, but what other explanation is there? A witch must have aided him."

I shrug and consider how desperate a witch would be to side with rogues. If this were true, something disastrous must be happening in his or her life to force her allegiance with them. That's the only thing that makes sense. No one would *willingly* do this.

I stare at the ground, kicking the loose soil with the toe of my boot. We're standing exactly where I fell, where I struggled to crawl away. I can see the imprints of my fingers in the earth. I shiver and glance back at Jasik.

"I need to speak with Holland. Maybe something in his

books will have answers."

Jasik nods. "Can I ask when he entered your vision? And"—he clears his throat—"why you didn't tell me about it?"

I sigh. "It happened weeks ago. It was before…before w-we lost them. And I didn't tell you because I honestly didn't believe it was true. It was weird, but my mind rationalized it to be just a nightmare, a figment of my imagination."

"You have to share these things with me, Ava," Jasik says. "I can't protect you if I don't know what's coming."

"I don't need your protection, Jasik. Quite the contrary, actually, don't you think? I faced him today, and I survived."

"Ava," he says, his voice low, warning.

I understand his unspoken words. I *barely* survived. Even worse, *he* survived too. But instead of admitting my faults, I play on what will undoubtedly be Jasik's weakness, because in these moments, I'm far too petty.

"I had another dream last night," I say. "You didn't just die this time, Jasik. You turned. *Rogue.*"

Jasik doesn't hide his shock. His eyes widen, his head jerks, his jaw falls slack. His reaction softens my heart and eases my nerves. Immediately, I feel like such a jerk for telling him right now, in the midst of a fight. But thankfully, he is as surprised as I was, and this only helps to solidify my feelings.

Jasik would *never* willingly turn rogue.

My vision was clearly influenced by my emotions. After weeks of watching him die, my imagination decided to join the game, and it doesn't play fair.

"I would *never*," Jasik hisses, mirroring my own thoughts.

But being the stubborn witch I am, I don't relax, because even though I am able to easily convince myself that that scene was no vision, there is still a nagging part of me that wonders if it's true. If Jasik wants me to be honest so we can talk about my visions, then I'll speak up.

"There seem to be a lot of impossible things happening in Darkhaven these days. Maybe this is one of them," I argue, crossing my arms over my chest in defiance.

"Ava, there has *never* been a case of a vampire turning rogue against his wishes. Never. It's impossible."

"Magic makes the impossible possible, Jasik. I think you're in denial," I say.

He snorts. "Listen to me. Please. It won't happen. I promise."

I soften at his words. He isn't promising he won't turn rogue. He is promising *me* that he won't leave. He won't abandon me like all the others have.

"I know. I believe you."

"You will need to detail all of this to Holland and describe the rogue to us. We need to know who we are looking for. I think it is fair to say we won't be patrolling alone anymore either."

I nod. "Understandable."

Nearby, the shuffling of debris catches our attention. We both spin, facing the possible attacker, weapons ready. Twigs snap underweight, and the brush shifts as an opossum scurries from its hiding spot in search of food.

Jasik and I remain so silent, so still, I am convinced the creature doesn't even notice us. After all, we are predators. It is prey. While it should be aware of its surroundings, we have so many advantages to ensure the cycle of life. Everything about us invites it closer.

I exhale sharply, easing the tension in my shoulders once I realize there isn't a threat looming overhead, and the opossum is alerted, growling and hissing as it runs away.

"We'll find him, Ava," Jasik says.

"I know, but until then, we all need to be careful."

"We should go," he says, his gaze still scanning the forest surrounding us, as if the wildlife is in cahoots with the rogues. "For all we know, he's still out here, watching us even now."

I know he's right. We must return to where it is safe—at our nest, among the other hunters—but I don't move. Not yet. There is one more conversation he and I need to have while we're alone, far away from eavesdroppers.

"Are you upset that I left without telling you?" I ask, already knowing the answer. Why do I enjoy torturing myself with these honesty sessions?

"I'm not upset," Jasik says. "I just wish you would have told someone. You risk too much."

"Don't you think it was time I rejoined patrols?" I counter. This is possibly the worst argument to make, considering there is a potentially vicious and powerful rogue vampire looking for me, but the words still escape.

"Only if you are *truly* ready," he says.

I know where this conversation is going. He doesn't trust that I am ready. With everything that has happened recently, and with the introduction to a new rogue vampire, I can't blame him for thinking I should confine myself to the manor. But that is all I have done since our friends died. I can't hide forever.

"I am ready, Jasik," I argue, tone firm. I need him to believe me even if I am internally questioning myself. But he doesn't need to know that.

"Do you even realize where you are right now?" he asks, gaze glued on me.

I frown, confused, but he continues before I can speak.

"Turn around, Ava," he orders. "Look."

And that's when I see it, where I am, how close I am to my former coven. I am a short walk away from the entrance to the backyard of my childhood home. I have hiked these woods most of my life. I know exactly where I am. I know how many steps it will take to get home from here, how I could hear my mother's call from this exact spot if she were looking for me. But somehow, I didn't realize where I was until he pointed it out, as if I were blinded by my own inner turmoil.

"No," I whisper. "I didn't realize I was so close."

Mindlessly, I walk even closer, taking the steps one by one. My legs feel heavy, as if the earth is pulling me down. Does it also want me to stop? Before it can answer me, Jasik grabs my arm, halting me.

"Don't, Ava," he says firmly. By his tone, I can tell how serious he is, and it is clear he has no intention of releasing me until I agree that returning home is a bad idea.

I jerk free, angry. "Why? Why are you so hell-bent on keeping me away?"

"It's not safe," he explains.

"I'm sure the fire has been extinguished." I don't bother hiding my annoyance.

"You have bigger things to fear than the fire," he says. "The humans are investigating. You can't become part of that."

"You think they would assume *I* set the fire?" I ask, shocked.

He shakes his head, his eyes softening. "Last night, while you were . . . *occupied*, Malik and I overheard them."

"And?" I ask. "What did they say?"

"And they assume the people who lived in that house perished in the fire."

"No one was there. My mother wasn't home," I say, still not connecting the dots.

"*You* were supposed to be living there, Ava," he says. "They don't know you left. They don't know your coven forced you out the night you were reborn as an immortal. If they believe you died in that fire and then you suddenly show up in town, the humans will ask too many questions. Questions you cannot answer without raising suspicion."

I don't speak, but silently, I can admit his concerns are valid. It's not like I could even be questioned. Maybe I could con my way into making them believe I was at a sleepover, but how will I hide my pale skin, my crimson eyes, my hunger? The moment they see me, they will know I'm *not* human.

"Being even this close to the crime scene is too risky," he continues. "For all we know, their investigators are patrolling the woods, searching the surrounding area for answers."

Jasik's right. I left the manor as soon as the sun set, and only a couple of hours have passed since I began my patrol. The humans could still be working, still trying to determine what caused the fire, what lives it claimed.

"I know. I'm sorry," I whisper. "But I have to see. I have to—"

"It's too dangerous," Jasik repeats, interrupting me.

"Wouldn't you go back?" I ask, irritated. Everyone in this nest seems too quick to judge me, but given the chance, every one of them would go back to save their families. "If this was *your* house, your *family*, wouldn't you need to see?"

He is silent. The seconds pass as he stares into my eyes. He's looking for something, but all he will find there is defiance. Still, he knows I am right. If this were his childhood home, he would return, but he would take it a step further.

He would insist on finding the person responsible. He would want answers. Most of all, he would want to locate his missing mother.

"She is still missing, Jasik," I say, reminding him of the most important part of this tragedy while desperately trying to keep my voice calm, even though a storm of emotions is raging within me. I am on the brink of running, but I stop myself. I try to remain grounded, rooted in place, because in the end, I need him. And I want his help.

Going back won't be easy. Seeing what remains will be a dagger to the gut. Even now, the blade is floating, and I must force it upon myself. I will need Jasik to withstand that pain. He has always been my anchor, and I need that weight now more than ever.

He sighs sharply and runs a hand through his disheveled brown hair. I imagine he left the manor as soon as he discovered I was missing, not even taking the time to ready himself for a fight. Sure, he remembered to grab a weapon, but he's still dressed in the joggers he wears to bed. His T-shirt is loose and wrinkled, and the grumbling I hear is his stomach, not mine.

"Malik is going to kill me," he says finally.

"He wouldn't dare," I say. "He knows how lucky he is to have you."

The walk back to my mother's house is quiet. The world is alight by the stars and the moon, but as I venture closer, everything seems to darken, as if even the earth fears what I may find. I know this should concern me—the elements rarely hide—but I never stop. Driven mindlessly toward the shadows, I am like a zombie in search of food.

I cross the threshold and walk into the backyard. I stare in disbelief at what remains. The house my father built, board by board and brick by brick, is gone. The shell of what was once a happy home is all that lingers. I wonder if Mamá has already seen the damage. Does it eat away at her too?

Jasik follows silently behind me, walking so close my skin crawls. I feel suffocated by his proximity, but the thought of losing his strength makes me uneasy. I know he is worried about me, about my reaction to what I am seeing. Maybe he thinks I will faint at the sight of everything I have lost, or maybe he fears I will commit a far worse act of vengeance against the people responsible. He might be right to worry, because even though I am consumed by the pain of seeing my childhood home in such disarray, a burning fury is raging within me. It is born and fueled by the very fire that stole my childhood.

The flames had spread from the house and into the backyard, reaching all the way to the center, where our altar once was. Crafted from the trunk of a tree at least one hundred years old, the sacred space is gone. The relics we kept there were destroyed by its wrath.

I crouch, scooping a handful of ash into my palm. I suck in a sharp breath, letting the remnants of such a powerful place fall through my fingers like sand. The milky sphere used to harness the moon's power is shattered around me. My vision blurs, and when I squint, these particles become one again, but my hope is extinguished the moment I blink away my tears. These bits of iridescent crystal mock my anguish with their cruelty.

I glance toward the house. From where I kneel, I can see straight through to the street out front. No one is there, the nosy humans of Darkhaven and the inspectors long gone. The world is dark, and Jasik and I are alone to deal with what remains.

Staring into the front yard from a place where I should be hidden makes my blood boil. I shouldn't be able to see the houses across the street. I shouldn't fear that our neighbors are watching me, wondering what I am doing and where I have been. I should be protected in this space, hidden by the house and by the forest. The moon is supposed to be my sole witness.

I stand abruptly and dust off my hands, not wanting to move the altar's remains. When my palms are clean, I walk closer to the house and stop just before I enter what used to be my kitchen. Normally, I wouldn't be able to enter the kitchen from the backyard. Not unless I crawled through a window or burrowed through the wood siding.

To my left, the sliding glass doors, which once opened to the dining room, are supposed to be standing firm, but they too are destroyed. The ground is littered in shards of glass, some stained black by the intensity of the fire.

I step into the kitchen, bypassing the parts of the floor that have already caved into the basement. The house creaks in protest like it is angry with me. After all, it was supposed to be retired. Its work was done. But I am home now, and it must bear my weight once again, even in its desperate position.

I walk down the hallway and stop at the front door. But it isn't there. The threshold is protected only by bright-yellow crime scene tape in the shape of an unwavering X. I flick it with my finger, and it billows softly but holds its ground, as if it alone can stop intruders.

I glance over my shoulder at the living room. Like the rest of the house, the room is outlined by a few standing wood studs, but all are burned and almost unrecognizable.

With the walls gone, the pictures that once hung there are missing, becoming part of the rubble that cakes the floor. The room is in such disarray, I can't even spot the few family photos I would have wanted to keep. I tell myself Mamá took them when she fled for her safety, but there is lingering doubt. Would she have wanted to remember the family she lost to vampires—one by death, the other to immortality? I'm not so sure.

The furniture is also missing, either consumed by the fire and turned to ash or now part of the jumbled heap at the center of the living room. I remember all the holidays I spent in this room and all the coven meetings I attended. For a small space, my mother could squeeze in a large crowd and still provide comfort and warmth and happiness. The image of the harsh creature she became flashes before my eyes—a stark contradiction to the mother I once cherished.

I turn back, peering at the street. Still, we remain alone, but the flicker of a dim light catches my eye. There is movement in the house across the street, but I can't bring myself to care enough to hide, so I continue my assessment of the damage done.

The stairs at my right are completely destroyed. Even if I could use them, they would lead to nowhere because the upstairs has completely disintegrated. The roof has opened to the night sky, and the house is illuminated by the stars. Our bedrooms, our altar room, the storage area where we kept herbs and crystals . . . they're just *gone*.

I turn back and face Jasik. His eyes betray his anguish, and I am certain his pain matches the agony and confusion strewn across my face. Tears burn, but I hold them back.

I sidestep my sire as I walk back toward the kitchen. I run my fingers against the one wall that remains. The paint is streaked, the drywall tarnished by soot and blackened by fire, but it managed to remain intact. I suppose this wall is the only reason the entire floor beneath me hasn't yet collapsed. Still, it groans and wobbles, making me believe a strong wind or a hard rain is all it will take to crumble.

When I reach the hall closet, I find the door broken from its hinge, just like I left it the night before. Like the rest of the house, much of the wood is burned. I shimmy past it, finding the clothes that hung here also missing, and glance down into the darkened basement. Everything in this house is reduced to ash. A lifetime of struggle to provide everything we needed is lost to one moment of rage so intense, the elements were used. I think about that man the humans saw, and I wonder if he has come back. Did he watch his anger burn along with this house?

The memory of that night flashes before my eyes. I take a step closer to the place I nearly died, and I stare into the darkness. I can't see the bottom steps, but I was just there, cowering against the wall, struggling to breathe. It feels so distant yet so close. So real and raw and painful.

"That's where I should have died," I whisper.

I'm not speaking to Jasik specifically, but I hear him approach from behind. His movements seem cautious and slow, but he never touches me. Maybe he knows I can't bear it. I can't withstand the comfort of physical contact. Not right now. Not when I may burst at the seams with one simple brush.

"You weren't supposed to die here, Ava," he says softly. "You were stronger than that fire."

I shake my head as I struggle to breathe. My throat is dry, my eyes burn, my chest aches. Everything around me is crumbling or already gone—my house, my relationship with my mother. Even my connection to my sire is wavering. Because he doesn't understand. He doesn't *know* how bad it got, how I was forced to use the amulet to escape. If I tell him, he will be furious with me, and that is a reaction I can't handle right now.

So I don't respond to him. I just walk closer to the darkness, lowering myself onto the first step that leads to the basement quarters. Jasik cautions me, but I ignore him. He knows he can't stop me. The worst that can happen is the house finally falls, and even though I'm certain that won't kill me, I almost wish it would. Because I feel as broken and disheveled on the inside as this house appears on the outside.

"I am going down," I say.

Something in my tone must make him understand that this is not negotiable, because he doesn't argue. Instead, he follows close behind me as we slowly descend into the blackness. When we emerge, I notice several things at once.

First, the basement is almost completely intact, which startles me since I know just how bad the fire was down here.

Second, the smell is so awful, I gag, covering my mouth and nose with my hand to prevent my stomach from lurching.

Third, across from where I lay dying just last night, something is scribbled in the soot. I squint, trying to read the message.

I walk closer as my vision adjusts, ignoring Jasik, whose voice is growing increasingly concerned with each passing second. I am focused so intently on trying to read the message that I barely comprehend what Jasik is saying.

"Ava, stop," he shouts. "We need to leave."

I crook my head, lowering my hand briefly as my mind

processes what is etched in the floor. Without my hand covering my nose and mouth, the stagnant odor seeps in. The smell of rotting flesh overpowers my senses, and I hack the thick air from my lungs. As nauseating as the smell has become, I do not make the effort to retreat, because from where I stand, I can see the note clearly.

With striking accuracy among the rubble, the person who left this threat has made his intentions clear.

You're next.

With the bottom edges bleeding into the ash, the letters are long and slender, as if they were written with the tip of a blade rather than fingers. Each line is carved so deeply, I fear it will never wash away.

Numb, useless husks, my arms fall limp to my sides. My legs wobble and my knees throb. Gravity takes hold, and I fall to the floor, slamming against the dirt. My weight burrows into ash, and it cakes my skin, as if trying to claim me as its own, as if it also understands that I was supposed to die here.

I touch the message, running my fingertips against the soft soil. Even though I move with such effortless strokes, anger is erupting within me. It overwhelms me so quickly, so completely; I viciously tear through the words, swiping them away until the threat lingers only in my mind—my eyes will never again bear the truth of it.

As soon as I complete my task, eliminating any appearance of what that man wrote here, something shifts in the room. The air tingles and prickles at my skin. The heat intensifies, my lungs spasm, and a buzzing erupts from the silent shadows. The steady crackling of magic pops all around me. I am so fixated on the air, I neglect to see anything else. But Jasik, ever-focused and always watching, notices what changed, what I was meant to see.

Jasik gasps and curses under his breath. I glance back at him, seeing his eyes wide, his jaw ajar in a gasp.

"Ava, come to me," he orders.

But I don't return to his side, and he does not move closer to me. I turn back and glance up, following his gaze, shrieking the moment I see it.

"Mamá?" I whisper, my voice straining.

With tears streaming down my cheeks, I wail, crying so hard I can barely breathe and screeching so loud the neighbors should hear me.

But I don't care.

Because mere feet from the message I just swiped away, there is a mound of cremains. Beside the human debris now resorted to ash, there is the burnt remains of a woman. Her skin is charred and black, the red flesh beneath exposed and singed and angry. She is perfectly preserved, almost magically so, but when I choke out a breath, crawling to her side, she begins to decompose.

By the time I reach her, desperate to pull her close to me, to cradle her in my arms and protect her from the harshness of this world, she has dissolved, crumbling to ash and mixing with the others.

"Ava . . . " Jasik's voice breaks as he says my name, but I don't look back at him.

I burrow my fingers into the soft ash, scooping it up as if I can restore what has long since departed this earth. My tears streak the cremains, forming dark blobs with each hiccupped breath.

Last night, when I thought I heard their cries, I was right. I did. They were here, trapped in the basement, desperate for an escape.

Did they see me stumble down here while looking for them? Were they hopeful that I had come as their rescuer? Did they watch as I used magic to save only myself?

Jasik grabs on to me, yanking me toward him, and as he does, the cremains I held fall through the gap between my hands. They flutter to the ground, landing in a heap before me. But unlike before, when I mourned the loss of our altar, evidence of their deaths taints my skin in gray. I swipe at it, unable to remove what is slowly becoming part of me.

Jasik spins me around, and I burrow my face into the crevice of his neck. He wraps his arms around me and whispers something against my hair. His skin is slick with my tears, and every time I move, he holds me tighter and begs me not to look.

From the depths of my soul to the point of my nose, I am awash with grief. The pain is so raw, so completely unbearable, I am certain it will never release me from its clutch. It overwhelms my mind, creating a budding fury raging within.

I think about that man and the message he scrawled, and it gives me closure to know I will soon avenge my fallen.

And from the amulet dangling between us, nestled comfortably against my flesh, I feel my shadow-self smile.

SEVEN

I sit mute on the couch while Jasik explains to the hunters what happened at my mother's house. He and Malik are arguing, but I tune them out. I understand Malik's frustration at our recklessness, but we did it. It happened. Dwelling will change nothing. And honestly, I don't care to discuss the fact that we went back to my house. If I hadn't gone back, I would not know my former coven is gone or that my mother is . . .

I swallow hard. A knot has formed in my chest, and it is beginning to rise, looming ever closer to my throat. I know it will smother me. I will suffocate as bile spills from my gut, consumed by the wafting odor, struggling to breathe, just like them. Fire may not claim my body, but it certainly has my soul.

The reality that I am alone—truly, utterly, irrevocably alone—is settling in. The pain and anger and fear consuming me will never cease because there are few things more terrifying than spending eternity *alone*.

I understand Will's fear, his desire to find someplace he can call home, because standing at the edge, a vast abyss before me, knowing I am immortal, is frightening. My future is grim, the truth of that like a noose around my neck, slowly but surely stealing every last bit of my breath and sanity.

Someone sits down beside me and slides a hand beside mine. My palms tingle at the sudden skin-on-skin contact.

I have been staring at the floor for what feels like hours, so hypnotized by the grain in the hardwood, I didn't even notice him approaching me.

It takes every last bit of strength I have to react. I sit upright, correcting my slouched position, and crane my neck to the side so I can meet his gaze. I don't bother to attempt smiling or speaking. I barely acknowledge his presence at all, actually. The flicker of my gaze, the sigh of my heart, is all I can offer him.

Holland is beside me, face broken by his distress. His brown hair is messy and fluffed over to one side. His nightclothes are wrinkled and stretched, his shirt splattered with remnants of toothpaste. His eyes are blurred and cloudy, his skin pink, his nose puffy. His tears have streaked his pale skin in faint white lines. Without my heightened senses, I probably wouldn't even see them, but I focus on them now, desperately trying to consume his strength where our skin meets, like the leaching, parasitic vampire I have become.

But I can't. My powers don't work that way. I may be able to lean on Holland, but the strength to overcome my agony must come from within me. And right now, I'm not sure I can sift through the darkness to find the light.

Holland is speaking to me now. His lips move, his tongue flops around inside his mouth. I watch it move so effortlessly, so precisely, it nearly puts me to sleep. I'm exhausted from the tears wept, but the more I think about what happened, the harder additional tears fall.

They arrive as quickly as a flood, but I am still shackled to the seafloor. I suffer as the waves crash over me, pushing me deeper into the abyss. I attempt to withstand their brute force, succumbing to a greater fury. I know I am drowning, the anguish enough to fill my lungs as I cry out for help.

I turn away from Holland and stare at the floor again. I think he is still talking to me. At least, I know someone is repeating my name, but my mind is foggy and throbbing. It grows louder with each second that passes. I wait for it to become rhythmic, a slow croon edging me closer to hibernation or to death.

Holland squeezes my hand and caresses my skin with his thumb. He leans closer and whispers his apologies in my ear. Finally, I hear him. When he is this close, I can't avoid his honesty, but I can avoid the waves. His proximity pulls me to the surface, and I break free of that tension. He smells like cinnamon—probably from his daily cup of tea. His breath is warm against my cheek, his words brutal and vicious. They tear right through my flesh, piercing my heart.

I yank free of him, unable to withstand his emotional torture for a second longer. I may not be sinking into the depths any longer, but he has me rising so swiftly into the unknown that I am becoming light-headed and nauseated. I am desperate to find land, to rest my heavy bones on something solid and real. But I am floating among the clouds now, too far gone to rely on earth's gravity to keep me safe.

Resting my elbows on my thighs, I press my forehead to my palms. I am rocking back and forth, keeping my gaze glued to the floor, but all I see are my boots. Scuffed and covered in soot, they remind me of everything I lost, everything I witnessed today.

I still smell her decaying flesh. I still picture her raw, pink innards scorched by flames. Never meant to be bared, they were angry and inflamed. I still hear the sound of her cries for help, the screech in her voice as she called out to me for help. Had she not been hexed to live life as basic as a powerless human, she might have saved herself. She might still be alive. They *all* might be alive—if not for me.

Their cries are growing louder, so I focus on the floor, body shaking, fingernails scratching my scalp bloody. Tears splatter onto the hardwood, and my vision blurs. I try to blink away the muddled mess I have produced, but I can't keep up. With my distraction slowly escaping me and my heightened senses rapid firing, I am forced to partake in the conversation around me. I hear their concern, but all I want is to dip back into that murky darkness, where I am unable to decipher what is water and what are tears.

"I think I should give her something," Holland says. His words startle me, but I don't object. I don't even bother looking up.

"Like what?" Hikari asks, her tone unmistakable. "What can possibly make this better for her?"

"I meant I can create an elixir to help her sleep, that's all," Holland says, his voice stern. I imagine him rolling his eyes at her, but I don't care enough to see if I'm right.

The sound of shuffling around the room rings in my ears, but still, I never look up. Instead, I close my eyes, visions of my former house looping in my mind. I don't want to witness this. I want to be free of what I saw today, but I refuse to dishonor my family by neglecting to remember them. I have thought about my father so often, it is as though he is alive in my mind. Mamá deserves the same loyalty, even if she behaved atrociously toward me these past several months.

The couch shifts as someone sits beside me. I don't have to look up to know it is Jasik. The link that connects us also alerts me when he is near. My skin prickles, my heart hums, my core burns for him. He offers clarity, becoming my sole focus.

Holland releases my hand instinctively, and my sire wraps an arm around my back while leaning into me. I rest my head against his chest, listening to the steady beat of his heart. I find it soothing, comforting. It silences the noise in my own head. Jasik rubs his hand up and down the length of my back, slowly, softly, methodically, and each stroke brings me closer to peace. I close my eyes, letting the voices slip away.

"Is it possible to give her something for her memory?" Jasik asks, and my eyelids flutter open.

"Is it fair to steal that from her without permission?" Hikari counters.

They talk about using dangerous magic to influence my mind as if I am not here, sitting silently beside them. The fact that no one considers asking *me* what I want angers me, but I don't bother speaking up. I suppress my frustration, letting it boil until the hunters make their decision.

"Hikari," Malik warns, voice firm.

"What? Maybe she wants to remember," Hikari says in a huff.

I appreciate Hikari's defense, but she's wrong. I don't want to remember, but I *need* to. I must. With my coven gone, no one is alive to remember them—no one but me, that is. And while I would offer my life's blood to forget the massacre I witnessed in that basement, I wouldn't dare invoke such dark magic to rid myself of the memory. My coven is a testament to how dangerous the black arts are. They were nearly driven insane by it, and now protecting their creation is my burden to carry.

A sickening thought occurs to me: as much as I worry I will be alone for all eternity, I know that's not true. The evil *thing* tucked carefully within the confines of my amulet will be with me until the moment I die. The amulet at my throat wiggles against my skin, and I know the creature inside is thrilled by this thought.

"She doesn't want to remember," Jasik says confidently.

"You don't *know* that," Hikari argues. "Being a sire doesn't make you a mind reader."

"How bad was it?" Malik asks, ignoring Hikari's keen remark.

"The memory of what she saw today will haunt her forever," Jasik says simply.

I appreciate that he isn't sharing details, but I know this is a courtesy meant only for this particular moment. Later, he will explain what happened, in detail, long after I am fast asleep, my mind too foggy for my senses to wake me to the sound of his voice. Eventually, they will know everything, and they too will bear the weight of it—just not as much as me.

"As a solitary witch, I may not be part of a coven, but I agree with Jasik," Holland says. "If it was as bad as I think it was, this will change her."

"I assume that was his intention," Jasik says.

"Do we know anything more about the man the humans saw?" Malik asks.

"No. We were alone in the house. He was long gone, but . . . " Jasik says, trailing off.

The room falls silent. After a few unbearably long seconds, someone finally speaks.

"What is it?" Malik asks.

"Ava was attacked by rogues while patrolling," Jasik explains. "One got away. This happens right after her house burns down and her mother was killed? That can't be a coincidence."

"It's not," I whisper.

Again, the room falls silent. I sit upright, continuing to lean against Jasik as I wipe the pain from my face. I take several deep, slow breaths before I face them. All eyes are on me, and thankfully, the room appears to be patient, allowing me the time I need to gather my thoughts.

"I know he had something to do with this," I say.

"How do you *know* that?" Malik asks. "I agree that this being a coincidence is unlikely, but let's not jump to assumptions. We patrol nightly because rogues are a threat. It makes sense that you stumbled upon a few."

"Coincidences like *this* don't occur in Darkhaven," I say plainly.

"Perhaps not, but we need a bit more to go on," Jeremiah says, backing up Malik.

I meet his gaze, finding him standing beside Holland, who moved to the seat across from me as soon as Jasik came to comfort me. Holland offers a weak, apologetic smile, but I'm not sure what for. Is it for the death of my coven or for his boyfriend's pointed remark? Honestly, I don't know, and I don't care. There is so much pity surrounding me, I am finding it hard to breathe.

"This rogue was different," I explain. "He sired the others."

"Are you sure?" Malik asks.

His disbelief is clear in his tone, but I haven't the energy to convince him. He doesn't have to believe me. Like the others, he will find out soon enough how much stronger this rogue is than all the others we have faced. Eventually, they will all see that this rogue turning up in Darkhaven the day after my mother was murdered is no coincidence.

"*I'm* sure," Jasik says, cutting in, as if he alone could sense how desperately I needed that save right now. Maybe the look of defeat is etched into my face. I glance up at him, smiling weakly, hoping I don't look as resigned as I feel.

"That is a rare creature," Malik says. "A rogue who sires . . ."

"It is," Jasik agrees.

"That is a *powerful* creature," Hikari clarifies.

"He was," I agree.

"I'm shocked you survived," Jeremiah says.

I flinch at his words, even though his tone is neutral. I can't fault him for his harshness because his concern is valid.

Holland reaches over and smacks him on the arm, silencing his lover. Jeremiah feigns shock and discomfort, but he knows he is crossing boundaries. Ever since we lost Amicia, Jeremiah has been less willing to patrol with us. He worries about Holland, and I understand. I don't want to lose him either.

"I barely survived," I say. "There were two others I managed to kill first. The only reason I'm still here is because he heard Jasik approaching."

"I think it's best we patrol in pairs until we find him," Jasik says.

"Agreed," Malik says, nodding. "And Ava, I know how hard this must be for you, but any additional information you can give us about him may help."

I remain silent, replaying my fight with the vampire again and again. I feel his breath against my skin, his hands at my throat, his promise that this isn't over. I begin to shake, knowing there is so much the others don't know but unwilling to be the one who shares those intimate details. Instinctively, I reach for my throat, sucking in a sharp breath.

"He was able to force his way into one of Ava's dreams,"

Jasik says, speaking aloud what I cannot.

"*What?*" Holland asks, gasping. "That's not possible."

"It happened," I say quietly. I hold my chest, rubbing my hands over my arms, not meeting the gazes of the curious vampires surrounding me. Jasik's hand is firm at my back, grounding me in this moment. I'm grateful, for I fear I might float away.

"But that's absolutely *impossible*," Holland says. "Spirit witches harness a rare kind of magic. You need a special link to the astral plane in order to dream walk or to receive visions. Rogue vampires are severed from the magical world. They are soulless, unnatural creatures, the embodiment of true evil. It just simply cannot happen."

I sigh sharply, seething internally. "Fine. It didn't happen. I made it up, hoping to waste everyone's time and prolong a conversation I have no desire to continue."

I regret my outburst as soon as the words leave my lips, but I can't take them back. Holland winces, wounded, and I hate myself for being the cause of that lashing. Even if he was being a bit too academic, too serious, too unemotional about my situation, I know he meant no harm. If I expect to best this rogue, I need to remain calm, collected. I need to *think*, not react.

"I'm sorry," I say. "I know you all want answers. I do too, but we will get nowhere in our pursuit of them unless we can all agree that no one *truly* knows how magic operates. I used to think it was impossible to *create* a pure, evil entity, but I wear one at my chest every day. I think it's safe to say we don't really *know* anything at all."

Holland nods. "You're right. I'm sorry. I never doubted you, and I certainly didn't mean to make you think I did."

"I don't know what's going on," I admit. "I don't know why this person targeted my coven, and I certainly have no idea who this rogue vampire is or how he even knows about me. But he's real, and he will return for me. We must be ready for that."

I swallow hard, remembering that message scribbled in the ash, the one that appeared to be magically linked to the reveal of my missing coven. The moment I swiped it away, something happened in that basement. Jasik might not have felt the chill of the elements, but I did. I am almost certain magic was used to kill my coven, but if I believe that, then I can't also believe that the rogue vampire was involved. Because a witch and a rogue wouldn't work together . . . Right?

"Huh," Malik says.

The sound breaks through my thoughts, and I meet his glazed-over eyes.

"What is it?" Jasik asks.

Malik blinks several times, clearing his vision so his glowing, crimson irises better focus on me. I frown.

"Ava just noted something rather interesting," Malik says. "Something we haven't stopped to ask ourselves yet."

"And what is that?" Hikari asks, crossing her arms. Her tone is fierce, but when she glances at me, her eyes soften.

"*Why her?*" Malik asks, brow furrowing as his curiosity grows. "Why Ava? And how did he know about her? If he's new to town, someone must have led him here. But who? And why?"

"And when and where and how . . . " Hikari says. "We can ask all of those questions, Malik, but we are still no closer to figuring out what's going on or what we should do next."

"True, but this is where we start," Malik says. "This vampire knows you, Ava. *Personally* knows you."

I shake my head. "I have never seen him before. I mean, outside of that dream, I have never met him."

"That doesn't mean *he* doesn't know *you*," Malik says. "He does, and we just need to figure out *how*."

This was the last place I experienced her happiness. I know that is why my mind brought me here, to watch her at peace. I find comfort in believing she is not in hell. After her horrific actions on earth, I had my doubts about the safety of her eternal soul, but this gives me closure.

I watch them from a distance—forever the onlooker, never participating, even when I so desperately want to run into her arms.

They don't seem to notice me. That's how I know this is a dream. I am asleep, hopefully safe in my bed beside Jasik. The tea Holland offered me was spiked with an elixir to soothe my aching heart and troubled mind, but also, I was so mentally exhausted, darkness consumed my tired mind with little protest from me.

I stand in the shadows, on the outskirts of the field. The grass is scattered in colorful wildflowers, and I yearn to pick some, to form a bouquet for my mother. But I don't. I remain in the shadows, where I was always meant to be.

Blooming trees encircle this sacred space, and I lean against one for strength. In the distance, my family is together, happy and free of life's burdens—even if only momentarily. I know they won't see me from where I stand, even if they glanced my way. The brush is too heavy here. Nature protects me.

I am watching my younger self. She appears to be maybe four or five years old. I don't remember much from that time, but I know I was too young to understand how terrible the world is. Still, I would give anything to return to this moment in time, to be a smiling little girl who believed so full-heartedly that the world is beautiful.

The sunlight is warm against her skin, illuminating her tanned complexion. She wears a dress with thin straps that cling to her shoulders. I watch as she shivers as the breeze caresses what is exposed.

Barefoot, she snakes blades of grass between her toes, the wildflowers tickling the sensitive skin there. I still remember how that felt, how the giggle, so full of life and joy, erupted from my chest.

That little girl believes she is safe, and she has no idea how the simple act of a setting sun will soon alter her life forever.

I know I am dreaming because *Papá* is here. He is alive and well, just like Mamá.

I have watched this dream unfold many times, and it always begins this way. It tortures me with memories of things I will never again have.

My father looks at her, at the innocent girl I once was, long before bloodshed became my sole focus. His jaw is strong, sharp, as he smiles widely. A dusting of hair covers his chin—some black, some gray. His forehead is creased, his eyes soft with lines etching his content state. This was the last time he was truly at peace.

"*Te amo, mija.*" His tone is deep but gentle as he tells me he loves me.

I close my eyes, repeating the sound of his voice in my mind. I hear him speak these words as if he were just here, right beside me. I feel his embrace. I smell his cologne, like spices and herbs, candles and potions. I remember him to be as strong as a crystal yet as gentle as the breeze. He was always the calm to my mother's storm, just like Jasik is to me. Two halves of one whole. I remind myself that some people wait a lifetime to find this level of affection.

I look at the little girl again, and I see it, the truth in her eyes. She believes she will be safe forever. She doesn't know about the demons of the world or understand the warning from spirit, that growing sensation within her gut that was screaming at her to leave this place, to protect her father. She was too young to understand it then, too young to help him, too young to believe in vampires and monsters.

In mere moments, the sun will set, and they will hear them. The vampires. They are waking, planning their attack. They are hungry. They are not here yet, but still, from the edge of the forest, I can see them.

I focus on my mother. She laughs as she reaches over, tickling her daughter. The little girl is loud in her desperate attempt to brush away my mother's hands. Her chest is bubbling with excitement, buzzing joyously like the bees in this field of wildflowers.

I sigh as I watch them, leaning against a nearby tree. I rest my head against its rough bark, ignoring as it scratches my skin. A shiver works its way down my spine, tingling to my toes. I shift my weight from foot to foot, but the sensation never lessens. Still, I ignore it, distracted by the scene before me, consumed by the promise of one more peaceful second with my family.

As the sun sets, it casts the world in shadows. My parents frantically pack their bags, shoving toys into pockets and abandoning Tupperware of uneaten food. My mother grabs the little girl and lifts her into her arms. They are running, and even though I never move from where I stand as I watch them, I easily keep up with their pace, as if I have now become hunter and they are my prey.

My mother trips, and they are falling, tumbling forward. The girl's back slams against the ground, and she screeches. My parents shush her, determined to keep her silent, but she is crying now, the bare skin of her back shredded by the rocks.

My father drops our picnic bag as he helps his family to their feet, and I glance at it, knowing this is the last time I will ever see it. He left it there, and so did we. For all I know, it's still waiting to come home.

They hear it, the rumbling thunder I now understand to be feet smacking the earth. It feels like an earthquake, and for a moment, I believe the ground will split in two.

The vampires are closing in on us, and I see that truth in my father's eyes. He knows we have no chance. We are cornered. There are more of them, and they are stronger. He knows what he must do.

He forces my small, frail frame into my mother's arms, and I continue to sob, burying my face in the crook of her neck. She attempts to soothe me, but there is no use. My injury is all I can think about. I don't even realize this is the last time I will see him. I have no idea that vampires will change my life forever.

Blood seeps down my back, staining my white dress, and from where I stand now, I am enthralled, mesmerized by the patterns and shapes it makes in the fabric.

My father is speaking frantically to my mother, but his words are a jumbled mess. My little mind, foggy and tired, can't keep up with them, so I just lean against my mother, sobbing, praying the pain will ease.

The catcalls of the encroaching rogue vampires erupt around us. They have baited us, forcing my parents directly onto the path they wanted. Realization flashes behind my father's eyes as he bids us farewell.

My mother is crying, shaking her head so forcefully, I believe she will break her own neck if she continues. She grabs on to my father's arm as he turns to leave us, walking directly toward the monsters and away from his family.

In an attempt to keep him here, she holds on to him harder, digging her nails into his flesh, and he bleeds. I think no one notices. Not she, nor little me, and he doesn't even flinch. But the vampires howl. They know he is injured, and they now know exactly where he is.

With one final glance, he looks back at us, eyes heavy.

Mamá is transfixed by his wound, staring helplessly where he bleeds. She loosens her grasp, and he slips free.

The little girl in her arms turns back, meeting her father's gaze.

He says something before abruptly turning on his heels and running. He disappears into the darkness.

I trail his path until he is gone, and that was the last time I saw my father. Because he never came home.

But now, as an onlooker, I return my gaze to my mother. She is focused on her little girl, cooing softly, trying to keep her calm. She dries her tears and disappears into the forest, blurring until I see nothing at all.

Alone, I turn back to the path my father disappeared down. Night has befallen Darkhaven, the sky gloomy and dark.

"She cut him. She cut him, and she let him go," I say softly.

The small part of me that wonders if she did it on purpose is squashed by the much larger part of me that is beginning to think this is no dream at all. No longer plagued by spirit, I think I am back at that place, during this time.

You can still save him, a voice whispers to me.

I run. I follow him down the dark path toward the vampires, and I ready myself to aid him in this battle.

But I halt when I reach him, realizing I am too late. The trees surrounding us are on fire, and the ground is covered in ash. My father is held upright by several rogue vampires, who feed from every limb, every exposed inch of skin. He is limp in their arms, and I know his soul has long since left this earthly vessel.

The rogue vampire who drinks from his neck stops and glances up. He looks at me, head crooked, and smiles.

EIGHT

Despite warming temperatures, a shiver works its way down my spine. Patrolling the forest is exceptionally unsettling when hunting with a partner because there is only one reason not to go alone—and it is most definitely *not* a good reason.

Jasik reminds me that danger lurks around every corner, behind every brush heap, and even within the shadows. We may be together, but that doesn't mean we are safe. Without the confines of the manor, we are simply *bait*.

I trudge forward, sidestepping broken branches and decaying leaves never gathered after falling last autumn. This past winter was brutal. From freezing temperatures to several feet of snow, Mother Nature was not kind to our region. Thankfully, as an immortal, I don't have to experience the brunt of her wrath. Vampirism has many perks, and the inability to die from the cold is one of them.

I shimmy past a tree, scraping the back of my jacket against the rough bark. Jasik glances over, frowning at me, likely internally chastising me for being so loud, so careless in my pursuit of the vampire who haunts my dreams.

Jasik was hoping luck would be in our favor tonight and maybe we would be able to sneak up on the rogue we seek. But I know that will never happen. In fact, I am so certain of this, I would bet all I own that he is watching us at this very second, simply buying time until he is ready to make his move.

The thought that we are probably walking into a trap doesn't escape me. I mentioned it to Jasik, and I even wondered if we should gather the other hunters to properly ready ourselves for an attack, but he explained that we couldn't abandon the manor. I already knew Jeremiah wouldn't agree to join us. He refuses to leave Holland behind, so he is essentially our stay-at-home guardian now, forever remaining alongside his witch.

I don't blame him for desiring a more peaceful life with his boyfriend, somewhere far away from all this chaos. I would like nothing more myself because Darkhaven has never been kind to me. I will never escape. I know it has every intention of keeping me here, from birth to death.

Still, I pressed on, but when we mentioned it to Malik, I opened another can of worms. Our new leader wasn't keen on the idea of sending me out again so soon after discovering my former coven, but Jasik pointed out that I am needed. With Jeremiah on a permanent vacation, we are down a hunter, and we simply can't properly patrol with just three.

But now that I find myself hiking under the moon, stars lighting my way, I have the jitters. What should be a peaceful place gives me anxiety. I hate that the rogue stole this space from me. As a vampire, there are very few places I can openly be myself—the forest being one of them. I should feel protected around nature, at unity with the elements, but instead, I question everything about my surroundings.

"How are you feeling?" my ever-perceptive sire asks.

I smile, staring at the ground as I maneuver through a tricky spot where a tree collapsed. It appears there is very little I can hide from Jasik. He mentioned he was aware that I was hiding visions from him and keeping secrets, but he never desired to push me to a confession. He wanted me to come to him myself, and while I appreciate the thought, that only makes it that much harder to look him in the eye.

Jasik is like no one I have ever met—honest and vulnerable, protective and loyal. I envy his strength. I'm not so sure I would have been as understanding if the situation were reversed.

I shrug in response, but he isn't looking at me. He keeps his vision cast ahead, scanning our surroundings, always readying himself for the inevitable attack. I think he plans to take the first hit and maybe even finish the fight himself, never needing to call on me for assistance.

He walks ahead of me, clearing the way so I can walk a bit easier. Today, we decided not to take the usual paths, which have had enough foot traffic just from us vampires that there is now a permanent walkway embedded in the earth, making for a relatively easy hike. Instead, we are leaping over brush and crawling around fallen trees. Every step I take makes noise, and I watch as Jasik flinches each time. On the other hand, he glides with experienced ease. I have yet to hear him snap a twig.

"I'm fine," I mumble.

"Are you sure?" he asks. Although he never turns back, I hear the concern in his voice.

"I would really rather not talk about it, Jasik. The whole point of coming with you tonight was to have a distraction."

I am snippier than I mean to be, and I watch my sire's back shudder as he winces at my tone. By now, he is probably used to my outbursts, but that doesn't make the impact any less a burden.

"I'm sorry," I say. "I didn't mean to sound so . . ."

I sigh heavily, not bothering to finish my thought. I have a bad habit of taking out my frustration on those around me, and I need to do better. I can't always be so rash and reckless. Amicia once told me she admired my persistence, my headstrong youth, but I am not so sure she would feel the same way now.

"I know this has been hard for you," he says.

I am too busy staring at the ground, watching where I walk so I don't continue making noise, that I don't notice he's stopped and is now facing me.

We collide, Jasik preventing me from slamming into him by clasping his hands around my arms and guiding me to a halt.

I glance up, meeting his gaze.

"Are you sure you are okay, Ava?" he asks. "We don't need to talk about what happened, but you seem awfully distracted tonight."

His concern is well placed. He fears what will happen when we finally locate the rogue—or when the rogue discovers us. A distracted warrior is a liability, and we are already out here alone, so far from the manor that I doubt the others would hear our screams. Both Jasik and I need to be at our best if we intend to make it home tonight.

"I promise. I'm okay. I mean, I hurt. All over. It's like a . . ." I exhale sharply, trying to find the best words to accurately depict just how horrible I feel. None come.

"It's like an anchor at your heels, pinning you in place, rooting you in a singular spot, even though you are desperate to run wild," he says. "And although the anchor is strapped to your legs, you feel the weight of this burden everywhere else. In your head and arms, around your waist, and atop your chest.

"Every breath you exhale allows it to sink a little deeper into your flesh until your heart is beating so brutally fast, desperate to keep your body alive, even though the blood supply to your extremities has long since been cut off.

"Everything burns, from your toes to your eyeballs. The pain is all-encompassing, and you are pretty sure, at this very moment, it is absolutely possible to die from a broken heart, even though your sanity scoffs at the idea. Because being generally healthy yet dying anyway seems impossible. But your grief is so powerful, so much stronger than your sanity, that your mental stability is easily squashed, replaced solely by your torment."

My lungs spasm at his words, and I release the breath I was holding. I suck in another sharp breath quickly, but it doesn't lessen the burn in my chest. My eyes water, streaks of tears dripping down my cheeks. I don't bother wiping them away.

"Yes," I gasp. "It's like that."

Jasik pulls me close to him, and I relinquish my entire weight onto his strong frame. With my knees weak and my legs like jelly, he holds us both upright, running a hand through my hair and planting kisses atop my head. He burrows his face in my hair, his breath warm and comforting against my skin.

I cry while leaning against his chest, allowing his shirt to absorb the evidence. I am shaking, and the harder I convulse, the tighter Jasik holds on to me, as if he alone can suck the agony from my pores and carry it himself.

When I am done, it feels like the night should be over and the sun should soon rise. I know that's likely not the case. After all, Jasik doesn't have a death wish . . . right?

Sniffling, I glance up at him, seeing for the first time how broken he is. His eyes swell with anguish—from the ache of losing his own sire or the misery of watching me break into pieces, I will never know. Because once again, words fail me.

I feel her magic before I even know she is there. It crackles, pulsating through me. The air tingles and thickens as it warms, my skin moist and slick. Long strands of dark-brown hair cling to my forehead, and I push them away, clearing my vision.

My chest is heavy with each long, slow breath I take. I try to speak up, to warn Jasik of what is coming, but I choke on the words.

As if sensing my condition, my sire turns back, but he is already several paces ahead of me. After our momentary emotional breakdown, we continued hiking until we were so far from our manor that I feared we would never make it back before sunrise.

Exploring an area of the forest I had never visited, I was eager to venture farther into the belly of these woods, but now I realize what a rookie mistake we made. Focused solely on finding the rogue vampire, we risked our own necks in the process.

"What is it?" Jasik asks, frowning.

I clutch my chest, feeling as though my heart is swelling ten times its normal size. Surely it will burst. It will consume every bit of my chest cavity until it presses against my ribcage, and it will explode, shredding flesh, spraying blood across the forest floor, soaking my lover in what remains.

"Magic," I hiss, watching as Jasik's eyes widen with fear.

The one thing we hadn't counted on was witches. Sure, we

have our feuds, but with my former coven gone, we assumed the threat from our mortal enemies died with them. We never considered the other covens of Darkhaven and how they might feel about that loss.

She emerges from the shadows, a wide grin split across her face, like she just caught us doing something bad.

Her dark hair is twisted into a tight braid, which flops over one shoulder. As she crooks her head to the side, peering at us through hooded lids, the braid disappears behind her. I hear it slide across her leather jacket, and the swooshing sound makes me cringe, almost as though she dresses like this to intentionally disorient her victims.

Her irises are so dark they appear black, and she narrows them at me, her gaze flicking to the pendant dangling at my neck. It probably looks strange, seeing a vampire wearing a black onyx crystal. If only she knew just how weird the situation actually is.

The thought occurs to me all at once: this stranger is a witch, and I am going to kill her. I don't necessarily want to, but if the choice is my life or hers, Jasik's life or hers, I have already made my decision. I don't relish the idea of harming a mortal creature, but I am fairly certain she won't give me another option. She is staring with death-dagger vision, and her blades are pointed straight at my heart.

She summons her element quickly, a fireball forming in the palm of her hand. She plays with it, bouncing it tauntingly up and down, from hand to hand. I can feel the warmth of it from where I stand, and it makes my legs weak. I imagine the heat of the flame licking my skin, the thick smoke coating my lungs, and I wonder if this is how my mother felt as she spent her dying breath calling for help.

I don't react to her presence, and neither does Jasik, though I feel his gaze on me. He wants me to decide, to choose whether or not this girl will live or die. She may be a fire user— one of the more powerful elements to use against vampires— but she is no match for our speed. I can close the space between us before she even makes the decision to flick her wrist to send her magic hurling toward me. I can feed from her before she can blink or snap her neck with minimal exertion.

But something stops me—the questions swirling within my mind. I have so many, and they loop endlessly. I fear they might remain there, forever unanswered, and I will always wonder if this is the witch I have been looking for. I am certain I felt magic that night, even if I can't actually prove it.

Regardless, the blaring truth of her appearance is hard to deny. *Why now?* Why is this stranger in Darkhaven? Why so soon and so suddenly after my coven was murdered? Did this mysterious new witch have something to do with the fire, with their death? I don't want to believe that. I want to give her the benefit of the doubt. After all, witches aren't usually confrontational by nature, especially not toward other witches.

But you're not *a witch*, a little voice inside my head whispers.

Anger is bubbling within my chest, and it will spill free. My pendant buzzes with excitement, catching the girl's attention yet again. I frown, wondering if she notices the entity contained within the crystal. The vampires never have, but they aren't connected to the elements the way a witch is, and luckily, my magical friend rarely makes an appearance while Holland is around.

"Hello, Ava," she says, and I suck in a sharp breath at the sound of my name.

"How do you know my name?" I ask. Immediately, I am on guard.

"I know your family," she says, accent thick and strong, like the magically infused air surrounding us. The elements hiss, springing to life. I squeeze my palms at my sides, a desperate attempt to control my raging emotions. I fear they may burst from me, shooting fireballs, ice shards, and air daggers in all directions.

"How do you know her family?" Jasik asks as he steps closer to me. He keeps his gaze focused on our visitor, never looking my way.

"When might be the last time you saw them?" I add.

We speak so quickly, our words blending together, a mumbled mess I am certain she will refuse to answer.

"*Nuestras madres eran amigas,*" she says.

The girl closes her fist, and the fireball dissipates. She takes several steps toward us, farther from the safety of the forest and closer to the danger of vampires. I am intrigued by her confidence, but I am also annoyed by her strength. It's as though she knows I won't hurt her, and I want to know why. That alone halts me.

"Our mothers were friends?" I ask, clarifying her confession that she knows my family.

I find it hard to believe because I have never seen nor heard about this girl before, not in pictures on the walls or stories from my mother. If she is lying, then this is an odd tactic. Does she think a former alliance with my dead coven will save her neck?

She nods. "A long time ago. They are more like acquaintances now."

I notice her use of *are* instead of *were*. Either she is smart to cover her tracks and use the present tense in speech, as if my mother is still alive, or she truly has no idea my coven was murdered last night. I am leaning toward the former.

"Do *you* know my mother?" I whisper.

My throat is closing, and I struggle to breathe. But I force myself to maintain my composure. I don't want her to think she has power over me when the truth is my current condition has little to do with her. Truth is, talking about my mother as if she is still alive feels like a thousand tiny needles piercing my heart.

"No, I never met her. Only my mother knew her," she says. "She knew your grandmother too. I've never met them."

Knew, the little voice at my chest repeats. *She* knew *her* . . .

"Who are you, and why are you here?" Jasik asks before I have the opportunity to call the witch out on her jumbled tenses.

"My name is Sofía," she says. "About two weeks ago, my coven was murdered by a vampire, and I have been hunting him ever since."

I gasp, disbelieving her at first.

She *knew* her. As in the past. Because she's dead now. Just like Mamá.

What are the chances that Sofía has also lost a coven to a vampire? Could we be tracking that *same* rogue? Is it even possible for him to kill her coven and come straight to Darkhaven to kill mine? The odds seem slim. And *why* would he be targeting entire covens? More importantly, what are the chances that two covens recently massacred just happened to be connected to *my* family?

"How do you know this vampire is here, in Darkhaven?" Jasik asks.

He shoots me a knowing glance before returning his gaze to the witch. Jasik only looks at me for a second, but his eyes say everything my mind is thinking. He will agree that the chances are slim, that this situation is an awfully rare occurrence, but the smart part of his brain—the one disabled in mine—will force him to find out the truth, for the safety of Darkhaven and our nest.

"Because a dark power is rising in Darkhaven," Sofía says. "And I intend to stop it."

Back at the manor, everyone is feeling antsy. It's not every day that two of us leave to patrol and return with a witch, bringing home a stranger, inviting a possible threat into the very place we slumber. But Jasik and I agreed we didn't have another choice. The sun was soon to rise, and we didn't want Sofía out of our sight. Not until we had answers.

"How long have you been privy to the fact that there are different kinds of vampires?" Malik asks, arms crossed over his chest. "From our experience, witches tend to group us in the same category."

Sofía smiles, leaning back in her seat, legs crossed. Malik is standing in front of her, towering over Sofía's much smaller frame. She doesn't seem fazed, as if a vampire interrogation is just another Tuesday night.

"I like to think my views are rather . . . progressive in my thoughts about the magical kingdom," Sofía says.

"'Magical kingdom'? That's an interesting way to put it," Jeremiah says.

He is sitting beside Holland, with one leg hitched over

the other, ankle resting on the other leg's knee. His foot is bouncing, the movement sending shockwaves down his leg and through the hardwood floor. They radiate up my own legs, tingling my spine. Holland reaches over, resting his palm on Jeremiah's thigh as if to calm him. It doesn't work.

"That's not an answer," Malik says, narrowing his eyes.

If I'm honest, I fear for Sofía's life. She may be a fire user, but she is surrounded by vampires, in an unfamiliar house, in a town she doesn't know. She doesn't have many friends here, and from my understanding, she doesn't have family either.

No one will miss her if she suddenly disappears. No one would ever know...

The thought, malicious and far more sinister than anything I thought I was capable of, comes to me quickly, and I gasp. The others glance at me curiously, and I look away, staring at the floor, ashamed of how dark my thoughts have become lately. The amulet at my collar burns so strongly, I have to grab on to it, easing the pain against my skin.

"The vampire who murdered my family was a particularly evil rogue vampire," Sofía says. I feel her gaze on me, but I don't look up to meet it. "And I don't wish to relive that moment."

"You don't have a choice," Malik says firmly.

Several seconds go by without sound. I look up, finding the two staring at each other, both waiting for the other to cave. Being an immortal, Malik has the upper hand here. He can wait forever for her to talk, and unfortunately, Sofía doesn't have that kind of time. Soon, she must realize that, because she exhales sharply, breaking their staring contest and forfeiting the title of champion.

"My coven was attacked by several vampires," Sofía begins. "At the time, I didn't know there was a distinction between the different kinds. I thought you were all monsters."

Malik nods his understanding. This is probably the start to every story ever told by a witch who now befriends vampires. Witches were all raised to think the same thing: vampires are evil. Simple as that. So determined in our mission to please our elders, we never thought to stop and ask if what we were doing was *right*.

"We were preparing for a ritual when they attacked," Sofía says, her story mirroring my own in such a horrific way. "That's the only reason we were *all* there. He picked the perfect moment to attack us. Any other time, I would still have family back home."

I nod, gnawing on my lower lip, desperate for her to continue. She glances at me briefly before returning her sights on Malik. I wonder if she knows my story. Does she know how Jasik saved my life, how he turned me into the one thing I feared most in the world?

"We fought. Everyone died. End of story," Sofía says.

"Hardly," Hikari says, finally speaking. "Not *everyone* died that day."

Hikari is standing in the doorway to the parlor, where we are all sitting and listening to Sofía recount the worst moment of her life. Although Hikari's stature is small, she still imposes superior strength, a formidable figure. Leaning against the doorframe with her head held high, she swirls a dagger in her hand, the easy effort of an expert killer. But strangely, Sofía appears to be unimpressed.

"I nearly died too, but a vampire saved me," Sofía adds. "That's when I learned that not all vampires are the same."

I glance at Jasik, who appears to be as shocked as I am. Her story mirrors our own so much it is almost offensive. Is she playing games with us? She must know how I was turned, and she is using my story to rattle us all. Unfortunately, it's working.

"But this vampire didn't turn you?" Hikari asks, disbelieving.

Sofía shakes her head. "He offered me blood to heal my wounds, but I refused. So he took me to our local hospital and left me on the steps. The staff found me bleeding out."

"And what about the vampire?" I ask.

She shrugs. "I never saw him again, but on the way to the hospital, he explained that not all vampires want this war. I didn't believe him then, but I do now. If he were lying, he wouldn't have brought me to the one place I would find help."

"This sounds like a fairly fantastical tale," Malik says. "Why should we believe it's true?"

Sofía narrows her eyes as she shifts in her seat, sitting upright. She swipes her braided hair over her shoulder and angles her neck. Carefully, she pulls her shirt down, exposing her skin—her tan, *marked* skin. Two puncture marks decorate the flesh there, pink and puffy but slowly healing. Based on these wounds, the timeline matches.

"The doctors stitched it up, and I told them I fell on a barbecue fork."

Hikari snorts. "They believed that?"

"Humans find it easier to believe outlandish stories than to agree that magic exists," I say.

Hikari rolls her eyes. "Whatever."

Hikari's anger and distrust is rightfully placed, and I know she isn't upset with Jasik or me, even if we are the ones who brought Sofía here. I sense her uneasiness, her desire to get rid of Sofía once and for all. That would make things a lot easier, but I doubt Malik would ever go for that plan. The thought that I am even considering it makes me queasy.

"What happened to the rogues who attacked your coven?" Malik asks. "Did the hunter kill them?"

"Hunter?" Sofía asks. "You mean the vampire who saved me?"

"Yes. Did he kill the rogues?" Malik asks.

She nods. "Most of them. The others fled."

"What about the rogue who bit you?" I ask.

"Coward," she spat. "He got away. Not a day goes by that I don't think about that moment, when he . . ." She clears her throat, eyes glossy. "I've been hunting him ever since."

"Do you remember what he looks like?" Malik asks, ignoring her distress.

She nods. "Of course."

"Describe him," I demand, voice breathy, desperate. I lean forward, hands clasped in front of me, elbows resting on my thighs. I *need* to know if we're hunting the same man.

"He, uh . . . He had no hair. Bald or shaved, I don't know. But I remember how smooth his skin was, like he did that on purpose, to make it harder to fight him. His skin was shiny and slick. I remember at one point, I tried to twist around, to escape his grasp, but his skin was dewy, and I just . . . couldn't."

"What else?" I ask. "Do you remember anything about his appearance?"

"He had a crooked nose and a lot of scars. I remember that vividly because I have never seen a vampire with scars. I thought that was impossible. Aren't you guys supposed to be fast healers?"

"Only if the wounds were sustained after his transition," I clarify. "If they happened before, the scars would remain."

She nods. "Yeah, I guess that makes sense."

"Anything else?" Malik asks. "Anything that might be particularly useful."

I don't miss the note of irritation in his voice, but Sofía seems oblivious. Or she just doesn't care if she's irritating a house full of vampires.

"He was tall, strong. His eyes were lifeless, just empty pits. Nothing was there. No emotion. No *nothing*. Just a monster in a shell. He wasn't anything like the vampires I faced before him."

"So you have hunted vampires?" Jeremiah asks.

"Of course. I *am* a witch. Hunting vampires is, like, my job."

The room chills at her words. True, hunting vampires is her job, but I think we're all hoping she has either retired or plans to rewrite her job description to clarify that she hunts *rogues only*. She hasn't attacked us yet, but I still don't trust her. I share Hikari's annoyance at this intruder, but I plan to be less obvious about it. After all, Sofía has something I need: *information*.

"And why do you think he is in Darkhaven?" Malik asks.

"Well, I don't know *for sure* if he is here, but I think he is," she says. "I used a locater spell to pinpoint magical surges, and Darkhaven lit up like fireworks, so much so the world map I used caught fire. I figured this place was my best chance of finding the vampire who murdered my family."

"*Rogue* vampire," Hikari says, making her intentions painfully clear. "The *rogue vampire* who killed your family. You are hunting a *rogue*."

"When was this?" I ask, ignoring Hikari's pointed remark.

"A few weeks ago," Sofía says.

I blink away the memories that flash behind my eyes, hoping my face doesn't betray my emotions. Because the magic her spell sensed wasn't the rogue vampire. It was me. A few weeks ago, I hexed my coven, damning them to life on earth as creatures little more than human. But I can't tell her this. As far as I know, Sofía is unaware of the existence of hybrids, and I intend to keep it that way.

"I think your rogue is here," Jasik says, changing the subject.

Sitting beside me, he leans over, grabbing my hand. He threads his fingers between mine, squeezing just hard enough to calm my nerves. I look up at him, vision clearing, the kaleidoscope of memories fading away until all I see is him, my sire, my lover. He gives me a knowing smile, and silently, we agree not to tell Sofía about my magic. Not until we must.

"Are you sure?" she asks, but Jasik is distracted, still looking at me.

"Ava fought a few rogues, and one in particular stands out as being your man," Malik says, answering for his brother. It appears we are all in on the silent conversation Jasik and I just had.

"If that's true, then you will need my help," Sofía says.

"We absolutely do not *need* your help," Hikari argues. "We are five experienced vampire hunters and one pretty damn powerful solitary witch. We can handle one rogue vampire."

At Hikari's outburst, Sofía glances at Holland, who stiffens. Jeremiah leans closer to him, wrapping his arm around his shoulders and pulling him close. Her gaze lingers too long, and Malik clears his throat, catching her attention again.

"It's been a long night, and I think we can all use some rest. For now, you can stay in a spare bedroom. Tomorrow—"

"Tomorrow, you can be on your way," Hikari says, interrupting her leader.

Malik sighs loudly and glances back at her, shaking his head. She softens slightly, but every time she looks at Sofía, she has death-dagger vision. While Hikari might be a bit harsh in her treatment toward this stranger, I can't say I'm upset. Truth is, I'm happy I have at least one hunter on my side.

Because something is off about Sofía. Ever since she arrived, my amulet has sprung to life, reacting to her presence every time she is near. More than once, I have caught her staring at it like she is wondering how hard it would be to snatch it from my neck.

NINE

My nightmare pulsates through me, shaking me awake. I lie in bed, drenched in sweat. Somewhere in the depths of my mind, my vision looms, like dark clouds hovering closer, the promise of a strong storm lurking overhead.

Images flash before me: the cry of my mother, the smell of smoke, fire, and blood. These pictures wrap around me, suffocating me, stealing every last bit of breath and sanity, until the lone rational part of my brain reminds me that I am safe now. I am *here*, beside Jasik, confined within the manor, among friends.

Except for one.

The cold splash of reality jolts me upright. Long strands of dark-brown hair stick to my forehead, and I swipe them away, running a hand through my tresses to clear my vision.

Sofía slithered her way into my dreams last night too, like a snake prepared to lash out at prey, but she wasn't alone. She brought a man—one who is certainly a stranger to me—and he clung to my shoulders, lowering his grip until he grasped my arms so viciously, he tore through my flesh. My screams were silenced, my mouth open but mute.

He begged me to be rid of the amulet, implying it is dangerous and that I can't handle what will come from keeping it so close to my heart. Even though the dream has passed, I still feel his desperation; it thickens the air, leaving a bitter taste in my mouth.

In the dream, Sofía told me to give it to her, and when I refused, she said she can help me destroy it. Unconvinced I can truly consider her an ally, I backed away slowly, ripping the man's fingers from my flesh and searching for my way out.

Still unsettled by the nightmare, I dangle my legs over the side of the bed, my heart hammering in my chest as I gulp down breath after breath. I feel the birth of an anxiety attack, and I try my hardest to squash it down, to save it for another day. Because with Sofía in the house, I need to be prepared for anything, for all the tricks she has up her sleeve.

Jasik is snoring softly beside me, covered by messy covers, arms outstretched above his head. He appears so peaceful, I don't bother to wake him. As much as I would like to believe this dream was a vision—because this would prove Sofía is evil and give the others the proof they need to cast her out of Darkhaven—I honestly don't think it was. I don't trust her, and my imagination knows that.

As much as I hate to admit this, it makes sense that she showed up in my dreams courtesy of my emotional duress. But not wanting to make the same mistakes, I jot down a mental note to mention the possible vision to Holland. His opinion will solidify what I do next—either I will ignore the nightmare, or I will bring it to Malik's attention. Holland will have to decide. He's supposed to be the expert here.

Even though I am fairly certain I have nothing to worry about, I can't deny the lingering doubt.

What if I'm wrong? What if it wasn't my imagination?

Sofía might have entered my dreams, intending to wreak havoc, which raises the far more important question . . .

How the hell did a fire witch worm her way into my dreams?

I tiptoe through the manor, beelining for the kitchen. The room is dark, and I don't bother turning on a light. At this point, I am used to my nightmares keeping me awake, forcing me up before anyone else. It's almost as though they are deliberately trying to drive me insane, stealing my sleep and sanity in one fell swoop.

While waiting for my breakfast to heat in the microwave, I replay my nightmare over and over again, deciphering the dream for any warning by spirit. But I find nothing peculiar, nothing except for the man, but the memory of him is getting fuzzy—like the longer I am awake, the harder it is to remember exactly what he looks like.

I sigh and think that this dream very well could be the product of an overactive imagination. It has all the telltale signs of being *just a dream*—the appearance of a brand-new foe, a fuzzy memory, little detail from spirit. Nothing more was discussed except for the amulet, and I already know it is dangerous. Being the guardian of anything comes at a cost.

The microwave dings, startling me. I grab my mug and exit the kitchen, making my way toward the solarium.

Outside, the night air is warm. I welcome the emerging spring season because I appreciate the smell of rain and flowers, but with summer comes longer days and shorter nights. Patrolling becomes more difficult, making my sudden encounter with this super rogue that much worse. If he eludes us well into the summer months, hunting him will prove particularly tricky.

Scanning my surroundings, I sip my drink as I walk into the yard. My gaze lands on the tree, the one that towers over the graveyard. The crow that was once perched on the tree's long branches, stalking me in the shadows as I confessed my pain, is long gone now, and hopefully, it won't be making another appearance anytime soon. As a bringer of death, it came for souls, leaving with many. Its work is done. I hope.

When I reach Will's grave, I plop onto the ground, tucking my legs under my butt and resting on my heels. I take another sip of the steaming blood, letting the thick liquid coat my mouth and throat. I lick my lips, moaning as I relish in the flavor. Blood smells nothing like it tastes. It has a savory fragrance but is sweet to ingest. I remember being repulsed by feeding. Now I remind myself that it could be worse. It could be brains.

"I bet you miss this," I say mockingly, immediately regretting my words. Will's death isn't funny, and joking about everything he can no longer experience is just plain cruel.

His headstone is covered in fallen twigs and leaves, debris having been blown here, settling after the last time I visited. I try to remember when that was, but I can't recall the exact day. It has been a couple of nights at least, and again, I am overrun with guilt.

"I'm sorry I haven't been around much," I whisper as I lean forward and brush his tombstone clean. I spill blood in the process, but the earth greedily soaks it up, as if it too enjoys relishing in life's essence.

I think about making a joke. Maybe I can make up for the last one that was said in bad taste. I could mention how spilling was intentional, a little treat for my fallen friend, but I don't say this. Instead, I just take another sip, closing my eyes as I bring the mug to my nose. I inhale deeply, slowly.

And then I hear it, the snap of something in the distance. A twig, a fallen branch, crunchy leaves left to decay, I'm not sure. But I know I heard it.

I open my eyes, leaping to my feet and spinning so quickly I lose all contents of my mug. I hold it out before me, like a weapon that could actually inflict damage, but I am alone. No one is here to experience the wrath of one hungry hybrid and an empty cup.

The woods blend together, trees morphing into a singular wall meant to trap me inside. I squint so I can focus better, hoping to peer farther into the distance.

Staring past the trees that surround the manor, I see no one, but the sensation that I am not alone never wanes. Instead, it grows stronger with each second that ticks by.

If I listen closely, I can hear the steady beat of a heart, but mine is pounding so loudly, I have to wonder if that is the heart I hear. Maybe it's mocking my fear like my bad jokes.

I take a step forward, intent on making a quick lap through the nearby woods, knowing that is the only way I will be sure that we are alone.

But something stops me. Movement at my left catches my eye, and I turn to see it.

Someone is watching me from an upstairs window. That window opens to the very bedroom that used to be Jasik's, long before he started joining me in my bed at night.

The curtain flutters again, falling back to its resting place as the shadow figure steps away from eyesight, and I slam down my mug so hard it shatters.

In Jasik's bedroom, I scour every shadow, every nook and cranny, every possible hiding spot she could have used, but I find nothing. I know what I saw, and I am positive the intruder was Sofía. Who else would be poking around Jasik's bedroom? Who else would spy on me in the cemetery?

Just as I'm riffling through Jasik's desk, trying to see if something is missing or out of place, someone walks into the room behind me. I know it's him without having to turn around, so I continue my search.

"Ava, what are you doing?" Jasik asks.

With a huff, I turn to find my sire watching me curiously, and the feeling of just being caught doing something really bad washes over me. I feel like a kid again, getting in trouble for sneaking downstairs on Yule or being caught with my hand in the cookie jar. While I know I have the best of intentions, I also know this doesn't look good. I overstepped boundaries by searching his room, and I'm not sure how he'll take that.

"Someone was in your room," I explain. "Do you notice anything weird?"

"Well," Jasik says, gaze scanning the room. He nods before returning his sights on me. "*You.*" He offers a coy smile. "That's pretty weird."

His easy, carefree walk over to me calms my nerves a bit, and when he rests his hands at my hips, pulling me close, I know he isn't upset with me.

"I'm serious, Jasik," I say. "I know Sofía was in here."

"Why would she be going through my stuff?" he asks, still amused, even though I'm trying to sound as somber as possible. I can't be the only one who thinks something is strange about her.

His tone agitates me. He seems far too happy and playful,

completely unbothered by the fact that our new houseguest was caught in his room. He never even asked me if I confronted her or what she said. Granted, I didn't catch her red-handed, and he probably assumes that since she's not still in the room with me, but I *know* it was her.

"There isn't much in here she'd want to take," he adds. "I have nothing but clothes and books. I doubt she'd want either."

"Maybe she was *looking* for something and checked your room first," I argue. "She could be searching for something in the manor that doesn't belong to you but belongs to *someone*. Maybe Holland's magic books or artifacts Amicia gathered during her long life. If she doesn't know *where* the thing is, she would have to check every room, including yours."

Jasik's smile widens so much it appears almost painful. He keeps his gaze on me, eyes hooded like he's still half asleep. He runs a hand through my hair, tucking strands behind my ears.

"What I wouldn't give to live in your mind for just a day," he whispers.

"I'm not making this up, Jasik," I snap. "I *saw* her."

I convince myself that wasn't a flat-out lie. While I didn't see Sofía specifically, I *did* see someone in this room. And if it wasn't Jasik, it had to be her. There is no other explanation that makes sense. The other hunters aren't going to randomly visit Jasik's room when he isn't there.

Jasik leans down, placing his lips against mine, and for a brief moment, my knees weaken. My legs turn to jelly, and my heart flutters in my chest. My stomach, growling from hunger, calms as butterflies swirl in my gut. The world slips away, and it's just us. It's just Jasik and me and the feeling of his body pressed against mine.

But then I remember.

I pull away, taking several paces back. We're both out of breath, and I wipe the evidence of my weakened state from my lips.

"We need to take this seriously, Jasik," I warn.

He raises his hands by way of surrendering, flashing his palms before me as he chuckles.

"I know. I'm sorry," he says, voice softening. "I'll mention it to Malik, see what he wants to do."

I nod, accepting his offer. When I asked, Jasik didn't mention anything was missing or out of place, so maybe Sofía was only here to spy on me, using this space as a window into my world. I might be overreacting, but even knowing she might have been just sitting there, watching me from the shadows, gives me the heebie-jeebies.

I shiver at the thought, and Jasik takes this as his opportunity to close the space between us, once again grabbing me by the waist and pulling me toward him.

"Now, where were we?" he asks, smiling deviously.

By the time I am done showering and dressing, everyone in the manor is awake. I make my way downstairs, peering into the parlor, where I find Holland and Sofía. Both are sitting cross-legged on the floor, surrounded by stacks of Holland's books.

Deep in conversation about magic and vampires and the history of the feud they both mention they don't agree with, they glance up as I stagger into the room, not bothering to hide my shock.

"What's going on?" I ask, narrowing my gaze at the sight before me.

Silently, I add, *Am I the only one who remembers this chick is a stranger?*

"Morning, Ava," Holland says, smiling.

Ignoring his pleasantries, I glance at Sofía. She meets my gaze, smiling widely. I don't know what it is about her, but we don't mesh well, even if she appears to be winning over every one of my friends. I feel a deep sense of discomfort when she's near, and I refuse to deny it. My gut is telling me something, and I will make the others listen.

I lock eyes with Holland and say, "We need to talk."

He frowns but agrees, apologizing to Sofía as he stands. He follows me into the foyer and out the front door. I close it behind me, spinning on my heels to speak face-to-face.

"Has everyone in this house lost their minds?" I ask.

"What?" he asks. "What are you going on about?"

"Did you forget that she is a possible threat?" I ask.

He rolls his eyes. "*No*, I haven't forgotten, but I'm willing to give her a chance. Benefit of the doubt and all."

"Does Jeremiah know you're cozying up with our new houseguest?" I ask.

Last night, Jeremiah didn't seem keen on the idea of Sofía sticking around, and just her presence seemed to make Holland uncomfortable. How did so much change overnight? It's like Jasik and Holland went to sleep and woke up two completely different people.

Holland scoffs. "I don't *need* his permission, Ava. I do what I want, when I want."

"Holland, befriending her isn't safe. Not yet. Not until we know more."

"Malik thought she was *safe* enough to sleep here, so I don't see the harm in getting to know her more," he says. "She could be a real asset."

"Malik stayed up the entire time to make sure we were safe," I argue.

The look on Holland's face confirms I must be the only one who discovered this.

After we'd all gone to bed, I waited an hour or so and tiptoed back into the hallway, ready to confront Sofía once and for all, but I only succeeded in stumbling upon a rather exhausted-looking Malik. He was seated on a chair directly beside the spare room door. He glanced up, frowning as I approached.

"Go to bed, Ava," Malik cautions. "You need to rest. We'll need your strength for tomorrow."

"Do you plan to sit out here all night?" I ask, crossing my arms over my chest. Despite the burgeoning heat, there is a chill in the air, and it makes my skin prickle.

"Yes, now go back to bed."

"What about you? You need to sleep too, Malik. We could take turns," I offer. "Split the shift in two."

He sighs heavily. "I'll be fine. This is my job, Ava. If losing rest is what I need to do in order to protect this nest, then that is what I will do. Now, go to bed.*" He emphasizes each word, the hard look on his face matching his tone.*

Reluctantly I tiptoe back to my bedroom. As I open the door, I glance back over my shoulder. Malik looks so tired, and his shift has only just begun. But I know he's in it for the long haul. Malik is one of the few vampires I know who would give his life in exchange for those he protects. That's why he is the perfect choice to lead this nest.

"If you need me, I'm only a few steps away," I say. "I'll be there."

He smiles, and it reaches his eyes. Only then do I realize how long it has been since I last saw him smile. Always on edge, always making the difficult choices the others dread to think about, I would argue that Malik has experienced the hardest burden since Amicia's death. I imagine taking her place is the hardest thing he has ever had to do. After all, she was his sire.

"Good night, Ava. Sleep well," he says as I close the door behind me and lock it.

Deep down, I knew something as basic as a doorknob lock couldn't keep out anyone in this house, but I'd slept easier knowing it was another obstacle in Sofía's way—should she decide to show her true colors and try to murder us all in our sleep.

"I didn't know he did that," Holland says, and I blink away the memory from last night.

That blanket of safety is gone now, replaced by a shuddering sense of worry that grips so tightly I can barely breathe.

I nod. "He did. Because he doesn't trust her. You shouldn't either."

"She might be an ally," Holland argues. "We can use another fire user."

"Maybe, but she needs to prove it first. She needs to gain our trust, Holland. We can't just hand it over willingly. And until she deserves our loyalty, you have to be careful. Be *smart*."

Again, he scoffs. "And how am I not being smart?"

"Just . . . don't get too close to her, okay? Don't leave her alone, don't share secrets, don't mention anything she can use against us. Assume she is the enemy."

Holland nods, huffing dramatically. "Fine. We'll do this your way. Is that all?"

I shake my head. "Actually, no."

Based on Holland's defensive nature, I think long and hard about mentioning last night's nightmare. I am not convinced he can approach this with a clear head, unbiased, but I don't want to hide it. I need the vampires to see I am willing to share this part of me, even if I only have bad news to share.

So I spill my secrets, and Holland listens as I detail last night's dream and what happened today in the cemetery.

"Honestly?" he asks, and I nod, holding my breath. "It sounds like your imagination is getting the best of you."

I exhale sharply. "I thought so. I mean, even now, I feel eyes on us."

I glance at the woods, noting how the trees cast shadows that move, shifting and changing in size every time the wind blows through the budding leaves. The sensation instills a deep-rooted fear, and the little voice in my head reminds me that I might be right. Maybe we *are* being watched.

"Then maybe we should get back inside," Holland says, but something in his voice tells me he isn't kidding.

Holland leaves me on the porch, but before I follow behind him, I walk to the edge of the steps, letting the tips of my feet hang over. I crouch down beside the gargoyle, resting my hand atop his head while keeping my gaze cast upon the woods.

The feeling that I am being watched still lingers, but I see no one in the forest. I slide my palm up and down the gargoyle's head as if to pet him, and I whisper for him to keep us safe.

Back inside the manor, I close and lock the door behind me, offering a sideways glance as I pass the parlor. Sofía and Holland are still there, sitting close together, smiling as they chat about magic, as if the conversation I just had with Holland was a figment of my imagination.

I remind myself that Holland is desperate for friendship. The sole witch in a house full of vampires can't be easy, especially when none of us truly understands what he is going through. Being a hybrid, I can relate to that sense of difference, to the desire to belong somewhere.

I have made the decision to mention my dream to Malik. Even though Holland's explanation makes sense, it doesn't exactly put me at ease. I worry he is too biased to properly analyze a possible vision.

I find the other hunters in the dining room. Hikari and Jeremiah are trudging into the kitchen, the swinging door between the two rooms swooshing closed behind them as they disappear behind it. Jasik is missing, but I assume he is still busying himself getting ready for the day. After all, we had a late start to the morning.

Malik is appropriately exhausted as he slowly slurps down a mug of blood. I consider telling him to take a nap, that we can handle the next couple of hours without him, but I know he will refuse. He takes his job as leader of this nest too seriously to risk something as benign as a nap.

He rubs his sleepy eyes as he glances up at me. We exchange knowing glances, but I never mention my offer. In fact, as I plop down beside him, I consider waiting to share my dream with him. The last thing his tired mind needs is another problem.

We sit in silence for a few minutes as I make a mental

assessment of my situation. I replay everything that has happened since Sofía showed up. Meanwhile, I don't speak, not until something occurs to me, and the realization has me stopping cold.

"Malik?" I ask. "Where were you this morning?"

"Hmm?" he asks groggily, not meeting my gaze as he stares at his nearly empty mug.

"When I got up, you weren't in the hall," I say. "Where did you go? I thought you were *patrolling* all night."

"Oh, yeah, I ended up going to bed," he says. "I stayed up as long as I could, but I figured you were right. There was nothing to worry about."

I sit upright, a chill working its way through my body.

"What do you mean I was right?" I ask. "I never said that. I wanted to share . . . *duties*."

I am quickly running out of code words for stalking and possibly killing Sofía. I worry stating it outright will upset the others. For some off reason, they are quickly growing attached to her and are far too forgiving when it comes to the act of this stranger. Sofía will see it as a threat—I can't exactly fault her for that *correct* assumption—and it'll start an argument. And right now, we need clear heads.

"Sure you did," Malik says. "Before you went back to bed."

"Malik, I *never* said that." My voice is screechy, and I struggle to control my rising fear. "I came out and told you to let me cover half the night. You said no."

He nods. "And then you went back to bed, and a little while later, you came out again and told me to go to bed. So I did."

"After I went back to bed?" I ask.

He nods and yawns. He finishes the last bit of his breakfast, smacking his mouth in disapproval as he stares into the empty mug. He seems completely unfazed by our conversation.

"We talked *twice* last night, Malik?" I clarify. "I told you I wanted to take a shift, and you said no. I went to bed, and you're saying I came back out again and convinced *you* to go to bed? And you listened?"

"Yes, exactly. Now, can you please stop talking?" Malik whines. "My head is killing me."

I sit back in my chair, silenced. I let the three conversations I have had today settle in, but the startling truth is hard to deny—something is wrong with my friends. They are acting weird. They are all emotional and vulnerable, trusting and dismissive. They are nothing like the careful, meticulous vampires who trained me to hunt and kill rogues.

"Malik," I whisper, a cold chill numbing my limbs. "That person you spoke to last night, *that wasn't me.*"

I quickly realize there is no use in explaining the truth to him. The leader of this nest, the one we lean on for support and strength, is gone. Like the others, he has been replaced by an easygoing pushover, and I know Sofía is to blame.

I know what I must do. I must consider this an act of war. Sofía has threatened the safety of my nest, and I will not let her get away with it.

"Good morning, Ava," Sofía says, the chill rushing bone deep.

Ever since Sofía arrived, something has felt off. The air is icy, even as the earth warms right outside these walls. I understand it now as the innate sensation instilled by spirit— the one that is meant to warn me of impending danger, of predator hunting prey. Except, in this scenario, I am not the hunter. *I am the hunted.*

"I thought it might be time we talk," Sofía continues.

My back is to her. I am facing the large bay windows that spill into the backyard. Several yards away, I can see the cemetery and then the forest, but I blink as I focus on something else.

I stare at her reflection in the window, watching as she walks closer. She is silent, so eerily quiet it is as though she is floating above the floorboards, hovering toward me.

I want to move, to stand, to face her head-on, but I can't. Frozen by fear or perhaps by the frigid air she brings with her every time she enters a room, my body is immobilized. My head is foggy and dazed, and I feel a single tear slide down my cheek. I can't even reach up to swipe it away.

"What have you done?" I hiss.

She smiles at me, but in the windows, her reflection is muddled. A thick, dark mist surrounds her figure, coating her essence in a black, frosty fog.

"Malik," I whisper. I glance at him, but he never looks up. He remains still, staring into his coffee mug, mesmerized by what he sees.

"He can't help you now," she says. "None of them can. In the end, we're always alone, aren't we?"

"What did you do to them?" I ask, angry, bitter at the thought that *I* welcomed this monster into our home and that everything that happens from this point on is *my* fault.

Sofía never answers. I return my gaze to her, staring at the window so long my vision blurs. I blink to clear it, but still, I can't focus on the witch behind me because my gaze has settled on something else.

Outside the windows and past the cemetery, something moves. The shadows themselves clear, forging a path for what lurks within the forest. Earlier, I felt something watching me, as I confessed my regret to Will, but I was distracted by Sofía and the idea that she is up to no good. Again, when talking with Holland, I felt that same tingle, the one that prickles my skin when I feel eyes on me. He brushed away my concern just as Jasik did. Now I know why.

Because at least a dozen sets of crimson irises are staring back at me, their figures emerging from the darkness of the woods. One rogue in particular stands out. The moonlight glistens off his shiny, smooth skin, sparkling against the thirsty, pearlescent fangs of his comrades.

I was right. The rogue would come back for me. I just didn't know when.

TEN

I scream, finding my strength and releasing a shriek so powerful, it shakes the house. Paintings and pictures hanging on the walls shudder, the vibration causing some to fall and shatter. The bay windows before me, perfectly preserved stained glass from the day the manor was erected, burst, shards of glass spraying into the yard.

The rogue vampires smile, relishing in my fear. Some even lift their noses, as though they are inhaling deeply, enjoying the scent of my fright. Terror smells a lot like metal. The unsettling, acrid odor irritates my senses, tingling my nostrils, a bitterly pungent scent. But the rogues seem to harness greater power from it, from the fear of death in their prey.

My bellow is enough to rattle the hunters, startling them awake from their spellbound slumber. Malik rises first. He stands so abruptly his chair falls backward, smacking against the hardwood so loud I cringe.

Jeremiah and Hikari emerge from the kitchen, mugs in hand. Their gazes scan the room, seeing the broken glass. The moment they lock eyes with the rogue vampires—still lining the forest as though they are waiting for us to make the first move—the two drop their cups. The liquid splashes, spreading like spiderwebs, each stroke intentional in its path, like messy finger paintings.

My vision lands on the cracked mugs, and immediately, I view it as a weapon. I imagine myself leaping forward, grabbing the largest piece, and stabbing Sofía in the neck, watching as she bleeds out, eliminating our problem once and for all.

The echoing sound of Jasik running through the halls catches my attention, and the vision of a dead Sofía at my feet dissipates. I hear him stomp down the stairs, unable or uncaring to be silent. Vampires are stealthy by nature, but today, no one is quiet, no one is effortless in his or her descent into this madness.

Jasik rounds the corner and enters the dining room just as Holland is stumbling from the parlor. I blink, and Jeremiah is at his side, pulling him close. Both look distraught, and I can easily envision the battle within the confines of Jeremiah's mind. Tonight, he must choose: protect his lover or obey his duties as a hunter. At first, the two paths will join as one, because killing the rogues will keep Holland safe. But there will be a moment, in the heat of battle, when the two paths will fork. I already know who he will protect. I don't envy him, because even though I am sure he will have no regrets, the guilt will still linger.

"What is it? What's going on?" Jasik asks, but no one responds. No one has to. My sire's gaze follows the wreckage, and he has his answer.

We are surrounded.

Seemingly unaware of the events that led to this moment—like how only seconds ago, they were all essentially comatose—the hunters leap into action, quickly arming themselves, readying for a fight.

I stand and face Sofía, preparing for my own battle, but I wasn't prepared for her shock. She looks past me, staring into the distance, mouth agape. She sucks in a sharp breath, her eyes wide and glued to the sight outside.

"You brought them here," I hiss, frustrated by her lies.

Sofía blinks several times before settling her gaze on me. She shakes her head.

"I—I didn't. I swear," she says.

"I am not fooled by your innocent act, Sofía," I say. "You threatened the wrong nest."

"Ava, you must believe me," she says. "I didn't—I *wouldn't*. I had no idea they were coming here."

I frown, considering her words. Something feels off about them, about her confession. I think about the strange way she phrased that.

I had no idea they were coming here.

I wonder what exactly that means, but I know there isn't enough time to properly interrogate her.

"They are waiting, Sofía," I say. "They are waiting for you, aren't they? For your order to storm the manor, to *kill* us."

Again, she shakes her head. "No, I swear! I'm not leading them."

This time, I can't deny her unusual phrasing, so I speak up.

"Then who is?" I ask. "Who is leading them? Who told you to come here?"

She begins to speak as if she might truly admit her wrongdoing to me, but something stops her.

"I don't know," she whispers, an obvious lie.

"I don't believe you," I say, seething. "And let me make myself exceptionally clear, Sofía. If *anything* happens to my friends, I *will* kill you."

I convince myself that wasn't an empty threat. Even

though I had my doubts, deep down, I was still hoping Sofía would become an ally. Holland was right. We could use another witch, especially a fire witch, but after the torment my former coven put us through, I refused to become a victim. So regardless of my concern over her loyalty, I planned to test Sofía, to make her prove she is friend, not foe. But it is safe to say she has failed my test.

"He is out there," Sofía says, voice hard. "The rogue vampire who murdered my family is here."

I nod. "He is, but I am fairly certain you knew he would be. Because you're working together, aren't you?"

"Stop saying that!" Sofía shouts.

The warmth in the room intensifies as she struggles to control her magic, but I never flinch. I stare directly into her eyes, daring her to make the first move—just like her comrades outside.

"Stop fighting with *me*," she says. "We have a bigger problem, Ava. We are *surrounded*. What are we going to do?"

"We're going to fight," I say plainly.

After we lost Will, Amicia, and the others, I learned a valuable lesson: *always* be prepared for war. Unlike the others, I am always armed, even if I plan never to leave the manor. Even now, I feel the comfortable weight of my dagger at my chest and the sleek shape of another blade at my hip. I unsheathe the weapon and hand it to Sofía.

"Now is the time you prove where your loyalty lies," I say.

Sofía glances at my palm, staring at the shiny metal. I offer her my backup knife, the one I started carrying after too many close calls. I can't always summon my magic to save me at a moment's notice, so I needed another knife. I relinquish it now, keeping the dagger at my chest, the one Jasik gave me many months ago, as my primary weapon.

Slowly, she grabs on to it, hand shaking, and tightens her grip around it.

"I thought you didn't trust me," she whispers.

"I don't," I say, emotionless. "But even though I am confident you will betray us later, I think you're smart. I think you will wait until the time is right, and based on your reaction, that time isn't now. And that means only one thing."

"What?" Sofía asks, voice cracking.

"Today, you will help us, because you need me to believe in you," I say. "You need me to trust that you are the person you say you are. The only way for me to have faith in you is for you to help us now."

"I am not your enemy, Ava. You'll see."

"Yes, I will see," I say. "They'll *all* see."

Sofía squeezes the handle of my knife so tightly her knuckles turn white. She appears paler than usual, her earlier confidence gone. If I didn't know any better, I might actually view her as a child, someone lost and broken, and not as the manipulative witch I have come to know.

"*Estoy asustada,*" she whispers. "There are so many."

I remain silent, allowing Sofía's confession to wash over me. She tells me she is scared, and I do believe her. I can see she is frightened, but I don't know *why*. Is it because there are at least a dozen rogues outside? Or is it because they ruined her plan by showing up early? Is she simply playing a fantastic game of cat and mouse?

Regardless, I still don't trust her, so if she thinks playing on my emotions will help win me over, she's wrong. My allegiance is to this nest—and she isn't part of it.

"Rely on your fire magic," I say. "It's a powerful tool against vampires."

She nods, eyes hooded as she stares down, unable to look away from the weapon I gave her. Her hands are tiny, and the weapon is even smaller. She probably thinks this is a trap, that a blade this small couldn't possibly pierce the sternum of a rogue vampire. I suppose she may be right. I've never had to use it. I guess she better have good control over her element.

"And Sofía?" I say.

She looks up at me, and suddenly I see how weak she looks, how childlike. There is an ache in my heart, but the feeling passes quickly. There are enough creatures in this house for me to worry about. I don't need another.

"Aim well," I warn.

Violence has the unique ability to affect all senses. From the sound of rogues combusting—a noise I have come to appreciate as the battle cry for Darkhaven. To the smell of blood lingering in the air, teasing my innards with the promise of sustenance. To the ash showering down, so thick I can practically taste the cremains of my enemies. To the heat of the flames, which lash out of me, scorching flesh. Everywhere I look, I see death and violence, fire and smoke, blood and ash.

I maintain my focus on the one vampire I care to kill. As I rush toward him, he licks his lips, a smile pulling the edges of his mouth into a menacing glare. But he doesn't scare me. Not anymore.

He lunges forward, a move I was anticipating, and I flip, twisting my body in the air, the tip of my boot making impact with the curve of his jaw. I land back on the ground, listening as my enemy howls in pain. Blood seeps from his mouth, and

I grin at the sight. I must have hit him at the perfect spot, tearing through flesh, as he bit down on his lip or maybe his tongue. He tries to wipe away the blood that coats his chin, but more pours from his wound.

He slices his arms through the air, fists balled, grunting loudly as he thrusts toward me over and over again, but I dodge each attack. I watch him as though he moves in slow motion, my heightened senses superior to his. He fumbles through his attacks, an amateur before an expert.

Unlike our last encounter, when he caught me off guard, I am prepared now. I knew he would come for me, and this time, I am not alone. While my friends slay the beasts he brought with him, he maintains his focus solely on me. Soon, he will be alone, trapped by my fellow hunters.

The rogue grows more ferocious with each failed attack, likely embarrassed to be bested by such a young vampire. His fists unravel, revealing fingernails sharpened to points, nail beds caked with dirt. He swipes through the air, and I move too slowly. His claws shred the fabric of my sleeve, but he barely reaches my skin.

My enemy smiles and licks his lips, thinking he has the upper hand, but he does not. He may be powerful, but he made the mistake all rogues make. They assume their brute force is enough to win battles. It's not. He lacks training, and I happen to have been mentored by the best vampire hunter in Darkhaven.

I distract him with a flashy attack, landing several hits, and he fumbles backward. He maintains his balance, but his frustration grows. He growls loudly as he again tries to strike me. Being several steps away now, I take this chance to withdraw my dagger and slice it forward.

My blade slides through his flesh like butter, leaving a devastating gash across his arm. He hisses, nostrils flaring. I do this again and again—each time inflicting a wound deeper and wider than its predecessor.

"Careful, blood loss can be a real bitch," I taunt.

Overconfident, I spin the blade in my hand, prepared to pull it down again, when the rogue speaks.

"I don't care if he told me to ensure your survival. I'm ending you. Tonight."

His words halt me, momentarily silencing that part of my brain that floods my body with adrenaline. He takes this as his chance to strike, and I stumble over my moves, carelessly missing my next attack.

Still processing his confession, I miss the moment he twists around, leaping through the air and landing behind me. Before me one moment, gone the next.

He grabs me by the arms, squeezing tight enough to crack bones. I yelp, screeching so fiercely the earth rumbles in response. I hold on to its wrath, beckoning its magic to aid me. But with each second that passes, I am overwhelmed by the pain in my arms. My grasp on reality is weakening as I relinquish my mind to the darkness.

The throbbing, blunt trauma to both my arms forces me to the ground. My knees slam against the hard-packed dirt, and I'm falling forward, unable to ease my fall.

My face smacks against the ground, my nose protesting the angle by flooding my lungs with blood. I hack, choking on the taste of my own essence. The liquid spills from my mouth, pooling around me, stealing my chance at preserving oxygen.

I hear the rogue laughing as I struggle to turn over, and I realize how close I am to dying. Without the use of my arms, I cannot defend myself. At least, not as a vampire.

I close my eyes, chest heavy, and I begin whispering, calling the elements, summoning them to me, but I am stopped so suddenly, I scream.

The blade enters my flesh over and over again, but all I can focus on—besides the voice screaming at me from within my mind, begging me to move, to survive—is the sharp sucking sound of my flesh grabbing on to the blade as it enters and releasing it as it is yanked out.

The attack stops, and the vampire is on top of me, rolling me onto my back. He straddles my weakened frame, leaning back so he rests his bottom on my pelvic bone. He slams his weight down hard, smacking against my body, and I wail. Each time he lifts his weight, he forces my spine to move too, and that simple act forces me to relive each time he sank my dagger into my back.

He leans down and grabs on to my wounded arms, digging his fingers into my flesh. He squeezes and shifts, grinding the broken bits of bone against each other.

"You thought you won," he says, chuckling.

Jaw clenched, I grind my teeth as I lean forward, ignoring every protest in my broken body so that I can touch noses with the rogue vampire atop me.

"I did," I whisper, finding strength in the look of horror on his face.

The subtle whooshing sound of fire igniting echoes in my mind. Almost immediately, he is engulfed in flames, from the soles of his feet to the top of his slick, smooth skull.

His screams blend together with the song in my heart, creating a pulsing, rhythmic beat radiating from the amulet at my throat. I find myself laughing as the rogue relinquishes his hold over me. And I begin to sway to the song only I can hear, waiting as the magic contained within the black onyx crystal heals my wounds.

The rogue vampire stands, stumbling backward as he frantically pats down his body, desperate to put out the flames. But there's no use. As soon as I lit the spark that ended his life, he was a goner.

He bursts into ash, fluttering through the air, floating down and landing atop me like confetti at a party. I notice how it sparkles under the moonlight, like glitter. I'll probably be scraping off bits of his cremains for weeks.

Ever faithful, Jasik is at my side. The others follow suit, but I glance past them, noticing that the rogues are gone— either by force or by retreat.

Sofía is there, standing over me, watching as Jasik snaps my bones back in place so I can properly heal. I cringe, wincing at the pain but never making a sound. If I'm honest, I like the way it feels. Never have I ever felt this alive, this . . . *free*.

Instead, I focus on Sofía. I smile at her, but she doesn't return the favor.

"What *are* you?" she asks, voice shaking.

I inhale deeply, the acrid scent of metal strong in the air. I lick my lips, never breaking eye contact with her.

And from the depths of the amulet, which aided me only moments ago, the entity laughs, and the sound, deep and throaty, escapes my lips.

ALSO BY DANIELLE ROSE

DARKHAVEN SAGA

Dark Secret

Dark Magic

Dark Promise

Dark Spell

Dark Curse

Dark Shadow

Dark Descent

Dark Power

Dark Reign

Dark Death

PIECES OF ME DUET

Lies We Keep

Truth We Bear

For a full list of Danielle's other titles,
visit her at DRoseAuthor.com

ACKNOWLEDGMENTS

Dark Shadow is dedicated to the readers who have picked up my books, mentioned Ava to friends, shared the series on social media, or requested local libraries and bookstores to stock it. I have been able to continue writing this series because of you. Even though I'm a wordsmith at heart, I'll never find the right words to express how much your support means to me.

So to the countless people who have given Ava a chance, to the many who have fallen in love with these characters and this world just as I have—*thank you*. Thank you for giving Darkhaven a chance.

As always, special thanks to the members of my Facebook reader group, Petals & Thorns; to my PA, Martha; to my writing cohorts, Shawna, Francie, and Heather; to my family and friends; and to my incredible publisher, for taking a chance on both me and my words. I love you all.

ABOUT DANIELLE ROSE

Dubbed a "triple threat" by readers, Danielle Rose dabbles in many genres, including urban fantasy, suspense, and romance. The *USA Today* bestselling author holds a master of fine arts in creative writing from the University of Southern Maine.

Danielle is a self-professed sufferer of 'philes and an Oxford comma enthusiast. She prefers solitude to crowds, animals to people, four seasons to hellfire, nature to cities, and traveling as often as she breathes.

Visit her at DRoseAuthor.com

CONTINUE READING
THE DARKHAVEN SAGA